THE HOBGOBLIN OF LITTLE MINDS

by

MARK MATTHEWS

Wicked Run Press
"The wicked run when no one is chasing them"
Proverbs 28:1

The Hobgoblin of Little Minds is a work of fiction. Names, characters, corporations, institutions, organizations, events or locales in this novel are either the product of the author's imagination or, if real, used fictitiously and not meant to be an exact historical depiction. Any character with a resemblance to actual persons (living or dead) is entirely coincidental.

For more information, contact: WickedRunPress@gmail.com

Edited by Julie Hutchings
Cover Art and Design by Vincent Chong

PRAISE FOR THE HOBGOBLIN OF LITTLE MINDS

"A wickedly clever take on a well-worn trope, The Hobgoblin of Little Minds explores lycanthropy through the lens of mental illness and shows Matthews at the height of his powers as a cartographer of the many shades of darkness that inhabit human minds. This bleak, Odyssean, and impeccably well-wrought fable proves what many of us have known for quite some time: Mark Matthews is the reigning king of modern psychological horror."
~ *Kealan Patrick Burke, Bram Stoker Award-winning author of Kin*

"Matthews is a damn good writer, and make no mistake, he *will* hurt you."
~*Jack Ketchum, Bram Stoker Award-winning author of The Girl Next Door*

"Matthews tackles contemporary fears head-on, and once you read his work, there's no escaping the emotional scars. It's unforgettable."
~*Michael A. Arnzen, five-time Bram Stoker Award-winning author*

"Matthews twists pioneering ideas from epigenetics and neuroscience into a classic horror tale, producing a nightmarish adventure that breathes new life into the werewolf legend."
~*Bill Sullivan, Ph.D, Professor of Pharmacology at Indiana University*

"A stunningly daring descent into madness. Dank, dark and scary as hell. Brimming with tragic characters and monstrous villains—think Nurse Ratched by way of Dr. Moreau under the direction of Cronenberg. This one is a belter. An absolute beast!"
~*John Boden, author of Spungunion and Walk the Darkness Down*

"Matthews delivers a shocking new asylum mythos. At Northville Psychiatric Hospital, longstanding literary horrors of tunnels, malign treatments, and twisted minds receive new Frankensteinian life, patched together into a frightful blend of existential dread and family entanglements."
~*Troy Rondinone, Ph.D., author of Nightmare Factories*

"As a new take on the werewolf story, it is a fascinating read, but as a deep dive into the realities of mental illness, the book is an absolute triumph."
~*IndieMuse.com*

"A foolish consistency is the hobgoblin of little minds, adored by little statesmen and philosophers and divines. With consistency a great soul has simply nothing to do. He may as well concern himself with his shadow on the wall. Speak what you think now in hard words, and to-morrow speak what tomorrow thinks in hard words again, though it contradict everything you said today."
~*Ralph Waldo Emerson, Self-Reliance*

1

KORI DRISCOE VISITS NORTHVILLE PSYCHIATRIC

Everything breathes, everything speaks, with a voice that fades but is never silenced.

Kori's dad had spoken these words in his manic state more than once, and she was starting to realize what he meant. She could feel the red brick ranch exhale in relief and give thanks as they emptied the house. For twenty-five years it had held such heavy burdens, but now all that was left was boxes of dishes and pizza crusts on a paper plate.

"I need to get out of here, Mom. You got everything done, right?"

It was a statement as much as a question.

"I wish you would leave with us tomorrow. Can't you just drive behind us?"

Kori dropped the box onto the floor with unspoken disgust. A boom echoed in the empty room, a cannon gone off, and she hoped whatever broken glass inside would cut those who tried to open it later.

"Don't act like I'm crazy for asking," her mom said. "You leave and I never see you. You won't come, I know it. You never do."

"I'll just be a few days after you. Look for jobs for me, okay? And remember, a Vet Assistant, or Vet Technician, it's called. I'm not a Veterinarian."

Mom was fishing for a fight and Kori was used to taking the bait. She eyed the front door, the oft-used escape route for this house when the walls dripped with tension.

"And don't open this box, something broke. You don't want to get cut. I'll open it when I get there."

Kori bent down to rub Hades' neck and then reached for the leash, letting Mom know the conversation was over. The aging bull-pit was eager to go, and seemed confused by the echo of her toes against the hardwood floor in an emptied house. Like her, she remembered days as a young pup, nipping at her dad like he was part of its litter and munching on his energy.

Dad's manic energy still filled the house even though he'd been gone for years. The last time Kori saw him was just a drop-off at the porch during the divorce. She had no idea it would be goodbye. If only she could've bottled up his fantastic flurry of enthusiasm and saved it for later, sipping on it when needed — but his bizarre rages and incantations that followed were a horrible aftertaste forever poisoning her life.

Dad's sickness wasn't the only memory that haunted this house. Years ago, Hades was attacked in the backyard and left with a gash on her hind leg. Her sibling, Hercules, was less fortunate. He was found bloodied and gored, his body dead but his eyes still open, looking up at Kori in shock and surprise — *how could you let this happen?*

A coyote was the likely attacker, the vet explained, maybe more than one.

Both dogs were adopted as pups from the Detroit Animal Rescue after Dad had woken Kori up at 5am, shaking her shoulder saying, "The dogs — *our dogs* — they're waiting for us. We need to go. Let's *go!*" Soon they were sitting in the parking lot waiting for the sun to rise and the animal shelter to open. "These are them," Dad said outside their cage. "See...these are *them.*" They were part of a litter rescued from a dog fighting ring, brought home to apparent safety.

But nothing was safe in this house.

Kori understood why Mom wanted to vacate with her new husband, but Kori was ready to fight, not flee.

"Your dad can find us in Florida if he wants to, you know," Mom said as if reading Kori's thoughts. "Even if he's in one of his *confusions*, he just *knows* and will find us."

Kori didn't argue the point, but gave Mom a hug and left her in the echo chamber. With Hades riding shotgun, she drove off in the Toyota Corolla, her dad's old car, one of the many things she took ownership of after years of his absence. She wore his old flannel shirts, soaked with his scent, she had piles of his old books, read the notes in the margins. Today she was wearing his University of Michigan hoodie.

Mom was right. Kori didn't want to go with her to Florida, and still wasn't sure if she would. She was looking for answers to help her decide, and driving to find them, taking the journey she always took in moments like these.

She pulled into the parking lot of Hawthorn Center, long term psychiatric care for adolescents, and parked on the fringes. Hawthorn was only a few stories high, but sprawled out at least 200 yards, with a fenced-in courtyard, a basketball court inside, and barbed wire on the top.

Shades were drawn on all the rooms, but lights still shone through the slits on the edges. She pictured the patients huddled in their rooms at this hour, having honest conversations, topics concealed and never spoken of in front of the staff. Hawthorn Center was named after the Hawthorn trees in the area but reminded her of the places she'd been to in the past.

Troubled kids like you are sent to Hawthorn, had been the threat. Well, she'd never been sent here. Instead she came here on her own, and was going to walk through the woods to the Northville Psychiatric Hospital, built on the same parcel of land, but closed and abandoned years ago. The place where troubled adults are sent.

The place where her dad was sent fifteen years ago, then never heard from again.

"I'll be back in a bit. Less than an hour," she whispered to Hades who sat on a blanket on the passenger side. She was speckled with scars where no fur grew from the night of the attack. Her ears were now forever perked in hypervigilance, frozen that way as if waiting for her attacker to show themselves again. Kori wanted to give Hades something she didn't have — trust that caretakers who love you always return.

With car doors locked and Hades safely inside, she quickly scurried into the tree line.

Tiny branches bent against her shoulders as she walked, deciding if she should be allowed to pass. The ground was carpeted by the crunch of leaves. Her lantern dangled from her fingers as she tracked through the trees. No need to light it just yet, for the moon shined with glowing fluorescence, a brilliant blue hue.

This area was dubbed The Evil Woods, one of many legends of the area. The trees tugged at her as if trying to stop her travels, but she knew the way through. She came upon a fence, newly constructed by the demolition company. Demolition was starting any day now and the abandoned hospital was surrounded with towering machines ready to tear it down.

Tonight was the last visit.

The fence had been cut weeks ago, but the metallic fibers took all her strength to bend, and when it finally yielded, she had to dart through before it snapped back in place. Last time the metal punctured her ankle and the blood squished under her foot with each step. That hadn't stopped her from spelunking into the hallways of the hospital and the underground tunnels. This desolate place felt like a second home, one that understood her on a level her own house never could.

With each step the buildings rose before her, turned alabaster by the moonlight. She scanned for silhouettes and shapes of others who might be here. So many times she'd seen shadows dashing to and fro, never sure of their reasons for coming, but they were certainly different than hers.

Red brake lights of a car circled through the parking lot. The guard had just made his rounds on foot. Now he was back in his car, the way he does for an hour or two after he walks about. There were more guards these days, as if fearful of the extra danger once the demolition started and the hospital was ripped open and disemboweled.

It didn't stop a steady stream of trespassers. She read their graffiti on the hospital hallways, crunched over the shards of glass from their smashed beer bottles, sometimes found a lit candle from a traveler just moments before her. More than once she'd heard feigned, mocking screams of terror echoing down the hallways, followed by too-loud laughter, from those who listened to urban legends that the place was haunted. Like the house she grew up in, it could never be fully emptied of its

9

trauma.

As she got closer, she felt the beating heart inside the brick compound go *thump-thump, thump-thump.* The past lives of the patients inside tugged at her chest. The building had its own gravitational pull and energy that radiated. She touched the brick, made one last scan of the area — no sign of life — then pulled the door handle, one of many entrances pried open over the years.

Her own entrance, her own reasons. She stepped inside.

The trapped air of the abandoned hospital surrounded her, each particle like it was alive, inspecting her skin.

Who is this intruder? Wait, we know who it is. You're his daughter. He was here for years. Please join him.

It took minutes before the air settled, before her breathing and heart moved in unison with the blood circulating through this place.

Accepted inside, Kori flicked the green Bic lighter and lit the gas lantern. Its glow brought the place to life. She'd brought flashlights in the past, but the beams felt unnatural, intrusive, making her just another security guard rather than a native of this land, someone who spoke its tongue. The lantern felt so right, evidence she was a friend, and each step she took brought the darkness of the halls into the light.

The first floor was a dark cave. Below her, the tunnels that connected these buildings were black as a tomb. On the roof was a suicide-proof deck, fully exposed to the stars, and tonight, certainly aglow under the full moon. She'd been through all the levels, breathed it all in. It filled her empty spaces, the loneliness she felt in her stomach and stuck to her spine.

To her right, she saw fresh graffiti on the wall and held the lantern to read the passage; *You Can't Scream with Your Lungs Full of Dirt* written in red bubble letters. She pressed a finger against the letter 'Y' and found the paint was dry. She'd come across wet paint often, trailing the artist by just moments.

A noise unnatural up ahead.

The quick patter of footsteps ricocheted down the hallway.

Another invader.

She stayed completely still, trying to hear better, but the noise vanished.

Just one person, Kori could tell, but fast and light on their feet.

She waited a bit before moving on. She wanted to be alone on her last visit. She stepped softly to avoid detection, but the crunch of her footsteps on rubble broke through the silence of the hallway. The crackling noises reminded her of thin ice she might fall through if her weight became too much. She walked past a plastic chair tipped over in the hallway and imagined who had sat in it last. She stepped on a discarded hospital smock that lay on the ground as if the last of the employees had to evacuate without warning.

The lantern light illuminated them all like a chunk of the moon had been brought inside.

She came upon a rusty old file cabinet that had been dragged by scrappers but then discarded when the effort became too much. Like every cabinet she discovered, Kori had already emptied its contents, ransacking for documents then folding them up into her backpack to examine at home in the light of her bedroom, as if translating ancient scrolls. She'd found inventory sheets, psychiatric evaluations, progress notes, some of it indecipherable from stains or from doctor gibberish, but all of it fascinating. Incident reports explaining why a patient was put in restraints or injected with Haldol to calm them down; just a small written history of the anguish here, the universes of thoughts in their heads, one Big-Bang expanding into a cloud of trauma.

In all her time visiting, she never found what she really wanted — an imagined dirty manila folder with "Peter Driscoe" written on the white label — and inside would be all sorts of psychiatry notes about how the man thought of his daughter, "Kori Persephone Driscoe" every day. How he missed her and wanted her to visit. She never found it in the written word, but imagined she could feel his presence through the asbestos-laced oxygen she breathed in, or that she could hear the bipolar buzzing sound that seemed to surround her dad right before he was hospitalized.

Dad's hospital stays always seemed to come like monthly menses. The first sign was his speech. He talked faster and faster until words ran into each other in nonsense, strung along with loose associations, speeding down a river full of rapids and rushing to the waterfall. He was awake for days, drinking coffee out of the white ceramic mug Kori gave him years ago for Father's Day, *World's #1 Dad* written across. The mood of the whole house lifted, as if from a tornado, getting sucked out of Kansas into the colorful splendor of Oz.

Kori missed that feeling. It had been torn out of her gut and left a gaping hole, but she did not miss the moments when the worst of the sickness took over. She could smell the bittersweet stench of his bipolar. It always seemed to hit in the early hours, 4am, full dark, brilliant moon.

At night, Dad would impulse shop. Amazon boxes would arrive in the days to follow, left up to her to return. He would start corporations through Legal Zoom with names like "Medusa Messiah," and made a webpage image of a Medusa head, snake hair a-blazing, photoshopped onto the crucified body of a bloody Jesus. The webpage was plastered with disjointed messages, word salad like; *"Look into my eyez. Feel the message. The hizz of the snakez slithering in the apple orchards will turn your heart to stone."*

Soon he'd leave the house to *spread the word.*

Police found him one time changing his car at an Avis because he was being followed by the Chinese. He was being poisoned. Recorded by *cameras.* Followed by *men.*

And it never lasted. It crashed down, depressions led to suicide attempts, mania to aggression, and hospitals took Dad through their locked doors. Kori and her mom waited to get summoned to one of the nearby hospitals where he stayed sometimes for three days, sometimes fourteen—but one time, at Northville Psychiatric, he was never heard from again.

She wondered if her dad felt safe here when it was open and running. If she just listened in the right spot, the message would come to her, she knew it. The noises of these hallways were the same thing she heard inside her own skull, her own inner ear. And as if the compound knew tonight was different, she could feel a thicker buzz of electric current zipping through the air. The leftover scent of suffering lingered.

One last message, one final SOS, since tonight was goodbye. Time to demolish this broke-down palace. It's not safe to keep it here, the city decided, but Kori feared little inside this place of dust and melancholy gloom, besides the random security guards with their sterilizing flashlights.

Bloggers and YouTubers loved to tell a different story about the danger here, spelunkers leaving here maimed, of hearing noises otherworldly, sounds unnatural. *I heard chains clanking, being dragged. I smelled bad breath. My legs got scratched with claws from little baby creatures who seemed like elves. They chased me away through the Evil Woods.* Each blog post trying to outdo the next one, demonizing the true hurt and sickness that used to live in these walls, bullshit easily seen right through.

Footsteps ahead.

The noise returned. This time zig-zagging for a quick dash. Someone hiding, moving from one shadow to the next. She was going to see them, and thought about calling out as she moved on. She knew the creaks of this place, knew the ruckus of high school revelers, or of couples walking slowly, hand in hand. The slow descent of the bricks settling, a bit deeper into the earth as the eons passed. She heard it all.

"Madness is but an over-acuteness of the senses," her dad had told her. "*That's Poe*," and then he moved on to other quotes too florid to discern, the tipping point when his thoughts spilled over into a howl.

She could still hear this howl from the night he exploded into anger and grabbed her by the arm and Mom called the police. Police tasered him when he ignored their commands, but it did nothing. They passed a bullet through his shoulder. That was the only time Dad had put a hand on Kori and it rushed everything faster down-current towards her parents' divorce date. Dad promised to 'get right' in front of the judge, but instead Kori saw him only a few more times before he decompensated again and disappeared into Northville Psychiatric Hospital.

And now Kori followed in these same hallways, years later, after Dad had been discharged into a "transitionary program" because the hospital closed. They couldn't share what happened to her dad because it was PHI—*protective health information*—and Dad had refused to sign for any information to be released.

Her memory of standing in the lobby once when the hospital was open was so vague, she often wondered if her mom was lying. "You went there once, remember?" her mom told her. "I tried to give you a visit. They refused. They only let you look around, and it was too much. I have kept you *safe*," her mom reminded her. "He's gone now. I bet they helped him and he's doing fine."

Rather than constantly scan the crowd of faces at coffee shops and grocery stores looking for her dad, she came to the last place she knew he'd been. Sometimes she went up to the roof to bathe in the night air, imagining the moon and burning stars tanning her skin, but tonight she was headed to the tunnels. No other area summoned her the same—the deepest part with the biggest pull. So she descended down into the depths.

The tunnels were built to connect the many buildings, to transport staff and supplies, and to move the heat through massive piping. They were the intestines where waste travels through. No windows, low ceilings, thick moisture clung to the dust, asbestos stirred up by scrappers who'd been taking out chunks to sell for scrap metal cash. She kept walking through the remains. The lantern was more brilliant down here, but could still only illuminate a few feet ahead. Every step she craved to see Dad's face in front of her, or hear the beat of his voice, but all she heard were deep, empty echoes—the sound of her own footsteps.

Following the pipes that ran like veins along the wall gave the illusion of moving faster than she was, like running down a hotel hallway. She ran the tip of her finger along the cement wall, kicking rubble down the hallway, dribbling it like a soccer ball with her feet.

After tonight her dad's memory would be buried, a chunk of her life taken away. They were demolishing her refuge, and she might be in Florida with her mom and miss the burial.

I don't want to go to Florida, I want to stay here.

Just like these buildings, Mom was slowly cracking apart. Kori didn't blame her for moving to Hollywood with her new husband. *Not the real Hollywood, the fake one — Hollywood, Florida. Not a real person, just a fake one.* Her mom knew Kori well enough to realize, Kori may never join her. The journey to the south felt like a refugee march, while walking down these hospital hallways felt like home. With each step she took down the tunnel, she was accepted by the dark that wanted to show her things the surface could not.

As if the building came to life, a flashlight beam shined from behind her.

The sound of someone moving with speed.

The security guard. He found me. He followed me.

Instinct took over and she dashed down the tunnel, lantern bouncing in her hand. Her thoughts fast-forwarded to being caught and her goodbye visit destroyed by a night in jail for trespassing, broken promises to her mom and broken promises to Hades.

She would not be caught.

The chase began.

2

KORI CHASED IN THE TUNNELS

"Don't run, don't fucking run," he screamed. "Just a bigger ass-kicking when you're caught. Don't run."

She ignored his command and took off in a frantic sprint, fueled by adrenaline. A pinball pushed by the plunger.

I've outrun more than you. I'm of this place below, your world is above. You have no stake here. I've beaten stronger forces that you. Teachers and police and psychiatrists could not contain me. I outsmarted and outmaneuvered them all.

But this guard was fast and gaining on her.

Her heart pounded like a drag race car piston. The sound of their chase bounced up and down the concrete walls. She sucked in air to fuel her legs, but his legs moved just as quickly and he barked commands at her to stop, warning that she was going to get hurt.

He wants to hurt someone.

Make some space, get ahead of him.

But instead of space, he was closing in.

Close enough to clutch at the back of her hoodie.

She flung an elbow and twisted. His fist-full of sweatshirt released, but he kept grappling and sprinting forward. She could almost feel his breath against her neck.

She knew this tunnel. She knew it as good as the veins she had traced on her wrist. As long as she could get to the open areas, she'd disappear into the Evil Woods. The woods would save her.

But she wasn't going to make it. He was collapsing over her, nearly running alongside, his words shouting to *stop* right beside her ear. She made some pivots and jukes, some last moves. Didn't work. His hands clenched again at her hoodie. She twisted and broke free but he was everywhere, the whole building was caving in, the last night here, her goodbye ruined.

Use his speed and size against him.

She slammed her back against the tunnel wall, planning on making herself paper thin, waiting for him to shoot right by and then she'd take off the other way, but rather than support her plan, the wall gave in. She tumbled backwards, lost her balance, stumbling down a passageway as if she'd fallen down the rabbit hole. She steadied her body and gained her feet.

The hospital was alive, it had helped her, opening a doorway to a skinny hallway.

How could she have not seen it before? It was not like the rest, a swinging door with no handle, made in camouflage colors to mimic the hallways.

She dashed down this new passageway, keeping faith it knew what it was doing, that her forehead would not smash into an unseen brick wall. Instead, it pulled her along faster, a slight descent as if going into a deeper Hell.

A terrible mistake. A gamble not paid off. He was still behind her, and no more space to evade him.

The tunnels hadn't saved her, they had set a trap.

His beefy limb reached around her neck and pulled her into him. She was caught. He had her in a full headlock. The man was thick and steadfast, a redwood tree from a truly evil woods, and she felt his muscles squeeze around her throat.

"Stop it you little fuck," he whispered straight into her ear with hot breath. "You're mine now. Stop it or you'll regret it."

But she wouldn't stop it, she would unleash all her hurt and rage and swing on this man like she swung on her teacher, like he was the heartless God of the earth above where stray dogs are stuck in dog fighting rings and dads are manic and mad and families are broken into sad little pieces.

Her limbs writhed around in such fury like she was on fire but she couldn't break her neck free from the headlock. She made a fist and pounded against his groin and felt her hand smash against the testicles. A resounding *oomph* escaped from his mouth but his stranglehold didn't give.

"Little fucking bitch," he grunted. "I should kill you. I *will* kill you. Nobody will know. Nobody will know."

The more she squirmed the tighter his grip clamped

around her neck. Her lungs burned for air that would not come. Her larynx was ready to break. She would join the spirits here after all. Her neck was snapping, her head spinning.

I'm sorry, was all she could think as she felt her life leaving her. She was trapped as if in a Toyota Corolla pounding against the glass windows but unable to break free, wondering where her owner was. She heard her mom at the funeral saying "I tried to warn her." He was squeezing her with such force that all her twenty-four years was about to break and burst out.

It did break and burst out.

A ferocious wail erupted as if a beast had leapt right out her chest. The walls of the hospital sprung to life with a howl. A shadow jumped. A golem made from the rubble attacked the guard.

The guard released her neck and Kori fell to the floor. Her windpipe cleared. She sucked air between coughs. Oxygen flowed to her lungs and then to her head.

The guard's flashlight lay on the ground and lit up rubble all around her. The hallway was shaking. The dragon roar sounded familiar. A dog whistle only she could hear, lubricating and loosening old memories.

The creature had his hands clamped around the side of the guard's head, squeezing tightly, lifting him in the air, weightless as a rag doll, while the guard's feet dangled below. He made indecipherable pleas, desperate squeaks against this huge shadow. Kori could sense the vice-grip of the squeeze tightening, felt the guard trembling, heard the crackling of his skull, until finally, the beast twisted his hands. The snap of his neck followed, and then what seemed like air escaping a balloon, *pfffffff,* his life being let out of his body.

The carcass tumbled to the floor.

Predator stood over prey, briefly, as if waiting for any movement, and when there was none, it turned to Kori. He towered over her, huffing through its nostrils.

His face in the shadows was Neanderthal, his body not really a human but some sort of pod grown from this concrete hospital, the sediments taking shape. The energy of his body made waves, one permanently slithering muscle, bulging and burning and never still, undecided. He peered at Kori through deep-colored eyes that blistered in the dark, black pinholes surrounded by swirling yellows and orange.

Kori lay motionless, waiting for her turn to be killed just the same, nowhere to run, just prayers that her mom would be okay, could live on without her, and that Hades would be found and cared for by a kind soul rather than returned to the dog shelter and then put to sleep.

She was trapped, just like her dad had been.

"Circular, circular, circular insanity. It brings you here, circling and circling and circling back. I left it in you, and you brought it back. You shouldn't be here."

She knew that voice, she had spent years with that voice, that scream. She'd heard those shrieks of rage, only now they were magnified and deeper and without even a trace of remorse. The face, though, seemed forever evolving, shifting right in front of her, as if wax and slowly melting. She remembered this person pacing her home at night and waking her in the morning. His square, firm chin remained, but his hair was longer than ever, a bird's nest covering his bushy eyebrows. The colors of his eyes had changed but the lids were still blinking in that same anxious flurry.

It was him.

Mom was right, her dad would find them.

"What did they do to you?" Her voice trembled, demolished by a larynx that felt cracked.

The beast stopped, cocked his head, like a slightly confused cocker spaniel, and then gazed into her.

"I feel you walk the tunnels of my head. I could smell it when you left your blood here. It's getting worse, that's how it happens. Then they put you on them, didn't they? The Depakote, the Lithium. You should know I came back for you once. You should know when it rains, the apples in the orchard wash themselves."

The sound she longed for, that Peter Driscoe remembered her, didn't come in a file, but came out of his mouth in a beastly tone, magnified by invisible surround-sound, like the tunnel of the hospital itself was speaking.

Her arms wanted to embrace him, but her hands disagreed and were grasping at the ground looking for a weapon, coming up with only tiny bits of debris, stones to throw at the giant. The sickness seeped out his pores and out his breath, a metallic tint to the air that she remembered had fogged up the whole house. A scent that came into her room as she slept, permeated her dreams, stuck to her clothes at school.

"Where have you been? What did they do to you?" she asked again. Even if she was his next victim, if she heard him answer, it would be a fair trade. For a moment, she felt his torment, his prison, his bones crackling and his body spasming as if being electrocuted and his soul trapped inside.

"Mouths to feed. Yours is not one of them. You shouldn't be here."

His shoulders were hunching and his spine bending, curving into something animal.

"Dad, it's me. You're here. I found you."

"That wasn't me. This is me. Get out of here. I've got mouths to feed."

"Feed? Who?"

"Mouths to feed, the *Vrykolakas*, I call them. Their necks are chained, and the other girl is coming. I can smell her. She's not like you. I tried to kill her before she had to suffer. She can't die, you can. Leave."

Kori wasn't going to leave, but readied herself to be grabbed by the neck, held in the air, and have her brain stem twisted until it snapped.

He didn't make that move. Instead he grunted, whined, distress that reminded her of Hades having a terrible nightmare, sprawling across the bed with every joint and ligament being stretched and fighting against a thought or desire unwanted.

I can save him. I just need to pull the right strings. Say the right words.

She clenched her fist and tried to speak with confidence.

"I'm not going unless you come with me. Come home.

Why are you still here?"

"You want to know why? I'll show you. Put you with them if you won't leave." He spoke with a guttural howl that made her eyes wince, the kind of voice that made Mom call the police. He bent down to scoop her up, his movements fast and fluid.

Inside his grasp, she realized this wasn't the dad she remembered — it was something monstrous. His fingernails like claws, grabbing the same arm he hurt years ago in the *final incident*. His body savage with bulging muscles. He was King Kong carrying Fay Wray, he was a shark pulling her out to the depths of a black ocean. She beat against his arms trying to break free.

"You think I hurt you once. That wasn't hurt. You see why you should leave when I say. When it storms and the apple tree falls in the orchard, don't take a bite." He walked deeper down the hallway, carrying her with one arm. She clutched onto the lantern as if it was the edge of a cliff, the only thing that would help her fight against the darkness.

And with one final grunt, huffing through his nose like a bull, he tossed her inside the room. She fell to the concrete like a piece of rubble, but before the lantern hit the ground, snuffing the light, she saw them. A snapshot photo with a burning image.

The room was lined with shelves, beds, storage, more like a medical room than anything she'd seen in these tunnels, like it belonged on the 5th floor. Not here.

In between, there were... *beings* chained to the wall. Their necks were twisted. Orange and yellow eyes swirled inside deep caverns, eager to see this gift being tossed to them. All of them just mutated humans. Noses like snouts, bodies completely naked, twisted sex organs, twisted limbs, movement distorted like their bones never grew just right but they'd adapted to their defects. Their mouths were opened when they saw the new visitor — they clearly liked visitors — and the chains clamored as they reached for her, knocking into bones on the ground.

The vision disappeared when the lantern dropped to the floor and shattered. The room faded to black, and she was in a sea of ink. A pool of black liquid all around.

Their chains clanked and she tried to slide away but moved right into one. It growled so primitively, she knew these were not humans. These were like strays found so damaged that no doctor could save them, only offer the sweet sting of the euthanizing needle.

She dashed off on the floor, an insect running for cover, as the creatures yanked against their chains. Their leashes would give no further.

Her back hit the safety of a wall but she was breathing too hard and wanted to stay silent. Hidden. Blinded by the dark, she could only feel their breath rattling in their lungs, their growls of hunger. She curled herself into a ball.

Though she couldn't see them, they could certainly see her, she was sure of it. Those eyes were meant to hunt in the night. She thought about pulling out her cell, but the blue light would just make her a target, and there was no cell service in these tunnels.

"These are the mouths to feed. Been stuck here so long, chained and bound, but I take care of them."

His words came as scents, triggering olfactory memories of times in the past when he spoke to her with a warm excitement, but in this dungeon, there was only coldness.

"They just ate, not so hungry yet. Don't get close. Pretend you're already dead like I do, then life don't hurt so bad."

This moment she'd prayed for, to find her dad again, had come true as a nightmare.

The ground was moist, the air frigid as her fruit cellar at home. She tested the darkness with a hand in front of her face. She could feel her fingers there, as if each cell was quaking, vibrating with its last bit of dying energy, but she could not see it. Only the slightest trace of light from the guard's flashlight down the skinny hallway.

"Dad. Please. You're sick. They're sick. Let me help. You got something wrong with you."

"Aye, there is something very wrong. That is why I stayed here and stayed away from you. Already hurt you once, and now I can't help it when the fire starts to burn."

Kori could hear them squirming, moving in their chains as if dancing to the beat of her dad's speech, making tiny currents in the thick, humid air. She moved her leg, just a bit, and a hand clutched her foot. She pulled against it, and the creature pulled back. A tug of war with her own body began, and she sensed the creature's agony, it's desperate hunger, and knew if she didn't break free the beast would eat her down to the bones.

After a grunt of her own, her foot broke free. She pulled her leg back and tucked it into her body. The creature yanked against its chain towards her but the leash would give no further.

It howled with displeasure.

"Dad, help me. Don't do this to me."

"You want me to be your dad, you stay here. This is the kind of dad I am now. I never let them down."

"What happened to you?"

"Trust the wrong people, you get hurt, carrot in front of me, stick behind. They made me burn so hot I forged a new kind of life from the flames, but they took her. Took my girl. She isn't like you."

"Dad. I know you're sick, but don't give up. We can be like we were."

We can be like we were. The words tasted of a lie, and she felt embarrassed for saying them. Maybe this *is* how they always were, the darkness of her bedroom at home, trying to save her dad from the monsters lurking all around—monsters that he'd been feeding.

Her back against the wall was cold but gave such comfort, an anchor, but to both sides of her was darkness, and in each moment, she felt one of the creatures would slide up against her and start clawing on her skin. She imagined one was inches from her face right now. An Alien with frothing mouth, and she was Ripley turning her face, trying to save herself from being eaten, waiting to fight back another day.

All it took was one wrong move.

Just listen for the clink of their chains and stay away.

"I did go see you once," Dad said. "I did come home.

23

After I smelled your blood. I know you cut yourself here and bled. I know you wanted to die. I could smell what you've been through. I went to your home, my old home. Traveling back like Odysseus after all these years. I stood in the shadows of the backyard and I saw him, *him*, your new dad, standing in the window, and knew that I could never be the kind of normal your mom needed.

"When the back door opened up and you let out our beautiful dogs, I had such joy, but when they came running out to the shadows, they feared me. Strange scent that I was, a serpent in the orchard. When Odysseus came home, his dear dog Argos could smell its beloved owner through the disguise after all those years. But not me. No sir.

"They surrounded me like the pack animals they are, like I am. When Hercules rushed at me, his bite felt like love, the special kind that comes from a sharp tooth in your flesh. The kind of love I gave you. God knows I wish I had laid down and let them protect you like they wanted to but instead I'm behaving like Cronus eating his own kids. That's all I am now, see, eating up you and then…

"I killed him. See. I did it. I tore him apart. Then I took a swipe at Hades and I left Hercules for dead. Makes my mouth water just thinking of his taste. That's who I am now. My other daughter understands, how getting a taste makes you want more.

"I know if I went back, I would have killed more of you, so I didn't. I stayed here. You shouldn't be here but now you are. We're a family again. This is the last stop."

Kori felt a wave of disgust, remembering the vision of Hercules in the backyard, bloodied and ripped open as if given an autopsy while still alive. Kori had given the animal a life full of affection and love, but it had all ended in horror.

Something in her knew it was Dad who had killed him all along. That's why she came here the very night after Hercules was killed.

Kori had visited this abandoned hospital after burying her dog, wanting to be alone, but instead she was spotted by a security guard outside who gave chase. She had dashed into the building, flew through the darkness with the radar of a bat, and headed up three stories high. She ran down a hall lit by slants of brilliant moon beams, and then popped inside a patient's old bedroom.

The guard could never find her, and she sat there all night with one arm resting against the rusty metal bed frame as if she were a patient and this was her room. She watched the spectrum of blue turn shades of aqua as the moon rose outside the window. She told herself she needed to wait until the guards were gone, but she knew the truth was she wanted a reason to stay here, to crumble along with these buildings, just as vacant, possessed by memories and hurt. All her efforts working as a vet assistant couldn't bring Hercules back from the dead, but it could help others.

That's what she did. She took care of things, and now mom wants her in Florida, but Dad needs her here.

Dad stopped talking but she could still hear the crackling of his bones, noises from inside his body contorting, like joints inside being snapped into something new. His body fighting against his words.

"Dad, let's get help. Mom is gone to Florida. The house is empty. We can get some food and I'll take you home and we can talk. Hades is in the car. Waiting."

"Going nowhere. I was meant to stay here, you see, taking care of them. *The Vrykolakas* are always hurting but I can take care of them. I feed them mostly venison and squirrel but sometimes a person or two. Ripped the flesh from the bones of those who aren't using it right anyway."

She wanted to scream, to bang on the wall, to plead to be let out, but nobody would hear except these creatures who've been here who knows how long, numbered in a dozen.

"A tree falls in the orchard one time—just one time—and it can't ever get up. Only reason I came here was to save you, you see..you see..you see. But you're here with me now, and now we live our lives together in the new way."

3

PETER DRISCOE, 16 YEARS PRIOR

His eyes popped open, head full of swollen blood vessels, each one ready to bust open and bleed.

Coffee. Cocaine. Something. *Need it fast. Need it now.* Something to bring the world up to speed.

Erection raged with blood, he needed to fuck. His spine burned.

The pillow offered nothing. The hotel room empty, his life was empty, his history full and could take no more. His eyes closed with head on the pillow brought no sleep, only dreams.

Let's go. Can I walk down to Asheville today and go to a poetry reading? Of course, I can. Why not?

The single serve coffee machine gurgled. The shades drawn on the hotel room, same shade cast since he left his family and gone mobile.

He gulped the coffee down scalding hot instead of waiting for it to cool. He imagined the black coffee turning the pink lining of his trachea into milky white blisters, full of puss, full of poison.

It was 5:16am and a layer of slime covered his skin. Pasty stuff covered his tongue. It was time to move on, so he gathered his two sets of paints, three shirts, and extra pair of shoes in his backpack and flipped it over his head. He patted his pocket to make sure he's got his wallet, and left out the door to walk. The *flame* inside started to fire, burning up his vertebra, zipping up his spine ready to explode out his head.

Wash it down. Wash it down.

He dug back through his clothes to the half pint of golden-brown whiskey, unscrewed the cap, then poured it down his throat to stop the flames.

Southern Comfort indeed.

Sweat exploded from his pores but then dried, soaked back inside his body, and he felt safe. His jacket was heavy, but that's good. He needed something to keep his insides from oozing out.

Don't let yourself explode from the inside, don't let the flame burn the fuse. It will try.

And don't go home. Never go home. Never go back. Not after last time.

His thoughts were screaming so loud, he needed more Southern Comfort to drown out the messages. Voices from shadows barraged him with thoughts and ideas, words floating inside the scents of garbage dumpsters that line the alleys where he roamed, hidden messages inside the chirps of birds landing on electrical wires that eye him with suspicion.

He can't escape the memories of the words Kori said, a sound forever tattooed in the air.

"I've seen how your veins bulge and your words growl, what's wrong with you, Dad? Your skin smells like it's burning."

So many moments of joy spent with her, but now she was afraid of the flame, she was hurt by the flame, so he took the fire with him and left.

Whatever you do, don't go home.

The sun was just rising, golden eyelids over the horizon, birds happiest at this hour, and together they sing the song of the universe. Words he understands and they pull him along the sidewalk.

Teachers are at school already. Some are teaching history, some who know how to bring history to life. They mimic voices from important figures, how they must have sounded, summoning them and breathing their words to a class and telling impromptu stories of imaginary families whose lives were impacted. *The people's history of the United States.*

That used to be him. He used to teach, and he lived off the energy of the students, but now he's on the run, moving as if a platoon of little beasts are right behind with sharp swords and hot torches. They smoked him out of his family, ready to gnaw at his thoughts and distort them, confuse them, turn them into things that can't be spoken.

Just move ahead. Keep moving.

Up in front he sees a white minivan waiting to turn down

the street, blocking the sidewalk. The car seems lost, afraid to move forward, and doesn't turn when traffic clears. He can feel its engine pulling at his chest. A woman and a beefy man are in the front seat as if in wait. The car door opens, and the woman appears. She seems both Scylla and Charybdis and he feels himself drawn to her.

"Peter Driscoe."

She knows my name.

"Peter Driscoe," she repeats. "Hear me on this. Picture this. You are home. Safely with her. It can happen. I can help you."

He's heard these lies before. He listened to them and he tried to follow what they said. He went home from hospitals and took the Depakote first, and then the Lithium, until his insides filled with cotton and he had no soul to love. No body to feel. No flame to burn, for his pilot light had gone out. Kori stopped loving him. Everything felt flaccid. He was a cold slab of fat, looking at Kori's eyes and the joy was gone.

So he stopped taking the pills and felt himself awaken. But the light inside turned into a searing flame, burning with constant agitation, and smoking with confusion. Everything that existed was unjust and he rallied against it. People were hurt. He had grabbed Kori's arm as if he needed to pull her from some wreckage, as if grabbing her arm and tugging with all his might was the only way to save her from eternal hell, the only way to pass along an urgent message of salvation.

His wife had stood by terrified. She called for help. The police came and shot him in the shoulder after the taser did nothing.

"Listen to me," the woman beckoned. "I'll take you to her. I'll make it so you can be with her again. Safely. She'll be proud of her father. You can teach history again. Come on. You're hungry and tired and you're looking for a place you'll never find. I can help you find it."

Her hair hung down and her eyes dazzled with comfort, like a mother's eyes, with secrets to soothe, her voice *knowing,* so *knowing,* but her promise was empty, like all of them, so he moved on.

He was done listening, but they weren't done with him.

He felt the man dashing his way, and knew he could turn to stop him if you wished, for in these moments his body has an outer layer, not confined by flesh, and he sees and hears things, perceives them in ways that the five senses lack, with a strength he fears to use. But he ignored the instinct to slam this man to the ground, and instead succumbed to the capture.

He wanted the relief of what was coming, hypnotized by the voice that *knew* about his girl, promises he still wanted to believe, and there was comfort in the sweet sting of the metallic needle they stabbed into his neck. His last sensation was being carried into the van, and the outside light going dark as the van door closed.

4

PETER DRISCOE AT THE HOSPITAL, DAYS LATER

The walls were painted in shades of pink and light blue, and the hospital piped in music meant to soothe but it certainly hadn't worked.

Driscoe remembered it didn't work, because he had fought. He had battled them all his last few days at Northville Psychiatric. He had waged war against the hospital staff, who seemed like gremlins and orcs and minotaurs. When the war was over, he found himself with bruises and pinholes in his flesh from the Haldol injections.

Something so fuzzy about hospitals, like he wasn't a person but just tiny specks of images inside a broadcast, put together with haste — but the reception was starting to clear. He lay in the hospital bed while the mania faded and the cold depression followed. His blood felt ice blue, same color as the walls.

His roommate wore hospital scrubs and Driscoe wished he'd put his clothes back on because he seemed like a doctor, like *one of them*. When they gave Driscoe his clothes back, minus one blood-stained shirt and leather belt (and no more shoelaces), he'd put them on. But not this man.

Driscoe wished he'd shut up, but instead the roommate kept muttering.

"Systems. There's systems you're not aware of running through us all the time. These systems. These people, these doctors, they *know* we *know*, so they're trying wash it out of our bodies. Just flush it right out. I try to stop from pissing so I can keep it in my head."

Systems, systems, he kept muttering, and his voice mixed in with the voices zipping around Driscoe's brain, finally fading from a manic scream to a saddened whisper, and everything turning cold and hopeless.

Look what you did, you stupid fuck. Driscoe cursed himself.

Got yourself trapped inside again. What the hell is this place? It's so big. Too big.

The roommate wiggled around in his bed, making his sheets crinkle. Days ago, Driscoe imagined dead skin cells stuck to the mattress coming back to life to eat him alive.

That delusion had faded with his mania.

With his mania gone, so was his strength and his fight, so they'd removed the restraints from the rails. His hands were free, the Haldol injections were over, but they still expected him to take their meds by mouth.

The medication cart rattled from down the hall. They were coming.

He was tricked to come here with the doctor's promise, but since that time, he'd only seen the doctor walking in the hallway, gazing at him for a moment, then breaking the look and moving on. He asked to see her, he begged to see her, but they said he needed to wait. How can he wait when he has places to go? He should be on the road, under the sky, instead of trapped inside. They got him like a dog catcher. He fell for her trap. Fell for the hope.

"Ain't so bad in here," his roommate said. "Been in worse, lots worse. You a lucky man, I hurt some real bad but not like you been hurting them the last few days. God damn you something. You'd be in jail if they couldn't call you crazy. The mental systems not as bad as the prison system, some say, some don't agree. You're like me. You'll live and die in this system."

Two staff entered the room. One large man with a beard so thick it hid his lips, and a bald head that showed the shape of his skull. Days before, Driscoe could hear his heart pump thick, fat blood, but now with senses dulling all he saw was just another big man.

These places, always with big men.

"Jankowski," the woman spoke.

Jankowksi got off his bed, straightened the pillow, and approached the nurse like a boy going to communion. He held the pills in one hand and the tiny cup in the other like it was the body and blood of Christ.

Watching him take the pills, Driscoe had his own reaction. Memories triggered of daily routines and daily decisions, always pondering if he should swallow the medicine. The tiny white soldiers had minds of their own and Driscoe always wondered, *Do they march for me or against me*? Driscoe could never find an answer that felt true.

"Doctor Herrick is to visit with you. Follow me,"

"See you, my good man," the roommate said as he followed the staff out the door.

"And Mister Driscoe, Doctor Zita would like to see you."

My turn.

Systems, systems.

Driscoe was followed by the staff as he walked down the hallway to the doctor's office, other patients shuffling back and forth, all of them lost inside this madhouse that was unlike any hospital he'd ever been. Endless hallways, so many floors, like he'd been abducted by an alien ship and scooped into a whole civilization living among the world but outside of it.

And he was finally going to talk with the head alien, planning to convince her that he needed set free.

5

DRISCOE IN DOCTOR ZITA'S OFFICE

"You ready to talk?"

"I've been ready. You made me wait."

"I apologize for the delay. I needed for you to stop fighting, for your mania to alleviate. You spent so much time in seclusion and restraints."

The blurred memories kept coming into sharper focus. He remembered his fist colliding with a few chins and some head-butts to noses. It was going to take some work, now, to convince them he should be discharged. He knew the drill with authorities such as her. He'd been placed on holds before, usually seventy-two hours, sometimes longer. He'd probably earned himself a couple weeks of an involuntary commitment with his rage.

This office felt different than the rest of the hallways, and the doctor looked at him like he was an exhibit in a museum, an artifact. He could feel the strange admiration. The badge she wore was crooked. He imagined her putting it on this morning. She was alone when she did it, he was pretty sure of this. She smelled of loneliness.

"You've made a mistake. I don't need to be in this fucking place," he said. "I got people. Places to be. You tricked me, lied to me."

"I did not lie. I told you truths that you were not ready for, but did not lie. I'm here to prepare you for truths. You can be with her again. You no longer have to suffer. We can help you with a different treatment."

Try not to respond. To respond just means more questions.

"You have nowhere to go but run. You can't keep running, it's time to stop. Your last few days here proved to me your power. Until now I've only read about it in old medical files. None of them can handle you, Driscoe. Your family, they can't. Your wife was there when you took the bullet, and that was enough for the divorce. But I see it as remarkable… I read the police reports."

"How do you know about that?"

"I told you, you were chosen for good reason. You know you're special, and that makes you feel cursed. You would not believe what I know."

This is going all wrong.

"When can I discharge?"

"We can discharge you soon enough, but not to the streets. I wouldn't lie about that, and wouldn't lie about being with your child. I know it's your daughter that drives you. She's still at the same house. I drove by there. I've seen the divorce paperwork, the child protective service interviews."

"Lies. Worse than lies, half-truths. Yes, she got hurt once. It wasn't right, I wasn't meant to spawn anything new. Her greatest hurt was being born."

Driscoe crossed his arms and found himself rocking in the chair. *Stop talking to her. This is what she wants. Don't engage.*

"Oh, we've seen you hurt people—just the past few days our staff needed medical treatment. You smashed unbreakable glass. Your mood is shifting now, waning and you're starting to feel lifeless. All that energy and power you had is only mocking you now that it's gone. The promise that manic power holds only leads to a deeper depression."

"I hate it."

"That's because you can't control it. You need to learn how to harness it. You've had the wrong treatment, always, again and again with foolish consistency. And it got you fired. Your history lessons plans at Edison High, I know about them. How you did a reenactment of the Iranian hostage crisis and kept students overnight. How you were supposed to teach World Religion but taught Mythology instead, and asked the children to name every god other than Jesus born on December 25th. They put you on paid leave when the parents started a petition and now you're out of a job, and even worse, you're out of a family. You have so much to teach, a different calling. I know this about you."

The doctor leaned in, elbows on the table, face craning forward as if to propel her words.

"Bipolar has the best of intentions, but the worst of results. I can help you change that. There is something in you that humans have lost. Humans were meant to hunt by the celestial moon with boundless energy and strength. Come with me, work with me, and let's find it! Turn you into a father again."

"I'm not going with you. I am a dead father to my child."

"I can help you return to her life. I've seen the best minds destroyed by treatment. Well, no longer. You just need you to agree. I have maybe a year to get you ready to leave, and if you agree, you can be part of our transition program. This hospital is closing, as you've likely heard. Here's what I want from you; be a part of our transition program. You'll get special treatment, you'll get out of here faster, and you'll feel like you've never felt before."

"How many lies you told these last few moments?"

"I'll tell you more truths than you will ever believe, and truth is, you've been mistreated. The world doesn't get you. I do. You and your doctors doing the same thing over and over again isn't the answer. 'Foolish consistency is the hobgoblin of little minds,' and I am here to kill your hobgoblins. Are you ready to try something new, instead of making it worse?"

"Sanctimonious psychoanalytical bullshit," he said, not towards the doctor but into the air, as if there were witnesses to the conversation. "You know nothing of what this is like."

"Here's a truth I am going to tell you. You tell me if this feels different. I know things about your daughter that you don't know. Things you suspect. I grew up with a parent like you. I *am* your child. Your daughter woke up each day and wondered what mood you were in. She needed to feel the temperature of your psyche before she decided how she was supposed to feel, how she was supposed to act. Before she knew if it was safe. She marveled at you quite often, your wit, your brilliance, your strength.

"Other times she was terrified. She asked why you were

sick. Worst, she wondered what she did wrong to make you sick. I know she found you after you tried to kill yourself. I know she visited you in hospitals, first with an eagerness for you to return home, then reluctance and wishing you'd stay. She's asked you to take your medication and watched you with such relief when the pills were swallowed down. I know all this because I did these things with my parent too.

"They say a son must bear the burdens of the fathers, but it's the daughter who cleans up the mess. My own dad left me when my mom got sick, said he couldn't do it anymore. 'You fix her,' he said. I couldn't fix her—but I think I can fix you."

Driscoe turned in his seat. He tilted his head as if it would make the words easier to hear by changing the angle of their delivery.

"There is no pill you can take that will stop you from not wanting to take pills. You know why? You feel the truth. You know there's something special in you that gets killed every time you take medications. It kills the best part of you. The part nobody understands. To be great is to be misunderstood. They marvel at you until they can't keep up. I am sure your wife couldn't keep up with your hyper-sexuality when you turn manic. Your mania is not a pleasure but an incessant hunger.

"Let's let it burn. Stop putting the fire out when it gets too hot. You know this. I know you do. Enough. Come with me. I have a place, there's another there right now, and we need you to join her. No lie."

No lie.

He took deep breaths, inhaled what she was saying, and her words tasted like truths. Should he trust his senses? His senses lie to him as much as any doctor ever had, and this doctor with her fair skin and her flattering words and gleam in her eye… It was nearly what he used to see when his wife looked at him.

He wished he could go sprinting out of the room, out the door, create a crisis in the hallway. He needed something physical, movement in his body to match his mind, and a fight with staff in the hospital hallway would provide such a release.

"What do you want from me?"

"Come work with me to sharpen your senses with new medicines. No more trying to stabilize your mood, we will make it sizzle. When this hospital closes most everyone will be transitioned back to the community. Funds for bipolar reintegration are ready for you. I can influence custody battles in the court, for…or against."

"Why don't you just make me? Why the fuck you need me to agree?"

"When you disagree with treatment, your brain will block things. I've seen men, not as powerful as you, but even more stubborn, and the treatment in our transition program… Well…it ended poorly for them. They didn't have your strength. If you don't bring all your strength and resources, if you are not fully invested, the same will happen. We need your full power and we need your buy-in. Come on, Peter, let's go. What do you say?"

Authorities. They're just people. Just people. So many times he'd told Kori that. They keep sending authorities your way, each one of them a new battle to face, and this one felt like some boss-battle that he was losing. Here he was, down to his last life.

"I say fuck you and fuck everyone here and fuck your lies."

God that felt good to say.

Dr. Zita had no words to reply, but instead pursed her lips and looked to her desk. She began shuffling papers, sat upright as if closing the chapter on a book and moving to the next.

"What if I let you see Kori right now? How would you like that? How long has it been? A year at least."

"I'll say it again — fuck you and fuck everyone here and most of all, fuck your lies."

"Not lies, I speak unspoken truths. You will learn that."

She began clicking on the computer mouse, then turned the widescreen monitor for Driscoe to see.

"We have been working on better closed-circuit surveillance, so I apologize for the poor quality, but here, have a look at our front lobby. I believe it will interest you."

The screen was black and white, certainly not crystal clear, but it was Kori on the monitor. Taller than before, the same jerky anxious movements of her head, always scanning her surroundings, not staying still, but it was Kori. Her hands were stuck in her pocket as if she held a secret inside. Black strands of her hair on one side of her head, the other side, shaven down to the skull. He used to love rubbing his palm up against the stubble just after it got shaved down.

Just seeing her brought a swell of warmth through Driscoe's chest. So many locked doors and walls between them, if only he could just reach through the screen and speak to her the splendor of words he's always hoped to say. Everything he had done in his sickness was just another way to scream her name.

"Imagine if she wasn't just visiting. Imagine if she was stuck inside a facility like this. I bet you would hate that. You've hated hospitals. I bet your daughter will too.

"Because, you see, your daughter has been having *issues*. Lots of *problems*. She's been expelled from school because she threw a chair at a teacher. She pulled a knife on her mom's first boyfriend... You didn't know about that part, but yes, there's a boyfriend, but he can't handle her either. I have her school records here. I have some mental health records. And I also have a petition. This is for a seventy-two hour hold to hospitalize her, same hold that you're on. Not here, over at Hawthorn Center. Next up is a sixty day hold. Then a 365 day hold."

He looked over the paperwork before him, scanning fast, eyes bouncing from the computer screen to Kori pacing the lobby, back and forth, reading sentences out of order, watching his daughter pace the lobby. The paperwork was his daughter's life before his eyes. Psychological reports, school records, divorce proceedings. The diagnosis was Disruptive Mood Dysregulation, and it stated she was *suicidal with a plan. Homicidal with a plan. Persistent self-harm with poor impulse control. Non-compliant with medications and an imminent risk to herself.*

Kori was in distress, that was no surprise, but a hospital would implant a chip of bitterness. It would kill her soul.

He thought of getting up and strangling the doctor until her face turned blue and she died right on that chair, but unlike days earlier, his muscles didn't have the energy. His rage couldn't be lit. She was just a psychological grifter, and she was not bluffing. He trusted that instinct.

"I have plenty of evidence and plenty of friends," the Doctor said. "I can have her put inside and convince any judge it's in her best interest. I am very persuasive. A judge has never denied me a petition for an involuntary stay."

Driscoe squinted at the computer screen, and there standing behind Kori was the beefy motherfucker, shadowing her. His arms waved wide towards the camera, making it clear he could scoop up his daughter at any moment.

"Your daughter knows you're here. Her mother agreed to bring her for a look around. Not to see you, of course, we explained that you refused to sign a release to permit visitors. But a daughter should know where her father is, don't you think? And before the sun rises tomorrow, she can be committed to Hawthorn Center, the adolescent psychiatric facility just over a mile's walk through the woods. Like father, like daughter, she'll grow up just like you."

Soon after, they wheeled him in a hospital bed below the surface of the hospital, taking sinister turns down hallways, then one final turn and a small descent into the skinniest of tunnels.

"Don't worry, someone else is already here. She's been here for months, going through partners, waiting for someone like you. Soon enough, you'll meet Maya."

6

2002 - MEET MAYA

An assortment of one-shot liquor bottles in a wicker basket sat on the counter. Packets of powder with *Maximum Sexual Performance* written across in neon letters were piled alongside. Butane lighters in the shape of skulls promised hot blue flame, made to sizzle a crack rock or smoke a blunt.

The party store countertop at *Owl's* was full of supplies that offered escape from the pain of living.

All Maya wanted was this pack of rainbow Skittles for $1.29.

The cashier counted out her change. Maya reached out her hand, palm to the sky ready to receive the coins. His white fingers flirted just above her darker skin. The cashier was afraid to let his skin graze against hers, she could tell. Her flesh was rich soil where a garden grows and new life springs forth, but he didn't see that. He saw something diseased and he wouldn't let his white skin catch whatever strand of germs he was sure was on her palm.

I wouldn't give it to him anyways.

He let the coins rain down to her hand and she caught most of the twenty-one cents in her palm except one dime that bounced upon the countertop, *ting, ting,* landed on the floor, and then rolled along its edge into the dirty tiles.

"You better get that, you're going to need it," Owl, the cashier, said.

She did need it. She bent down to pick it up, secured the rough edges of the dime in her fingers, put the change in her pocket, and carried the Skittles outside. She ripped open the top, chewed a handful and felt the rainbow explode in her mouth. She walked by men standing against the brick wall of the party store drinking bottles from wrinkled brown bags. One of them mumbled, "Psycho bitch walking."

She could feel their fear quake. They've seen her in all her *states*, bore witness after she was pulled out into the street and speaking words they couldn't understand, warning them to not mess with her, and when they didn't heed the warning, she beat on some who tried to stop her from taking flight. Men in uniforms came and scooped her up, took her to their places, clipped her wings that needed to grow back each month.

Someone was following her lately. Sometimes watching with cameras, sometimes listening through radio waves, usually inside the white minivan that crept along, or parked down the way. The heat of their eyes roasted her body as she walked deeper into the city's bowels, moving along the sidewalk, weeds busting between the cracks, mind rushing faster than her legs.

Her house had been boarded up after Daddy died and she didn't pay taxes, but she lived in the house just the same. She only had to pull back the wooden board, tagged with red graffiti, and push it to the side.

Sometimes she had to run off neighborhood dope fiends, them stuck inside, lost in this funhouse, not knowing the way through the hallways like she did. The house spit them out in disgust but always accepted her inside. The house was alive, with a mood and a mind and a red heartbeat. For the last few weeks she'd been laying in its stomach, curled up on a carpet full of dirty memories, hoping it would digest her. Waiting for someone to show up and take her body and burn it up to ashes so she could sit next to her father.

They came to get Daddy's dead body, why not mine?

But they never came for her. Didn't matter how long she lay there, dead inside. Soon enough the weight shed from her soul, the sleep was gone and she was fully awoke. Her brain started spinning like a tornado, gathering energy and lifting to the sky, so she took her money and got some Skittles and returned.

She found old cracker boxes laying in the house; Wheat-thins, Triscuits, and loaded up the fireplace. She lit the paper on fire and waited for old bits of wood stripped from furniture to catch flame. The cardboard went up fast and the smoke mixed in with the scent of her daddy's cigars, which coated the walls of the house.

She could still hear Daddy taking puffs of his cigar, coughing out smoke, then washing the coughs down by sipping his brown whiskey, ice cubes jingling.

After the first few drinks, right after his lungs exploded with coughs but just before the drink put him to sleep, he'd tell stories of her mom. How she gave birth to Maya after just seven months and left her in an incubator.

"Your mom waited for you to get home and then lit out for new territory. She was tired. So tired, and wanted to stay asleep, so she got out of this life altogether by her own hands, with pesticide. Poisoned herself, some say; others say she took the antidote for all that ailed her."

More drinks of whiskey came next, not bothering with a glass or ice anymore but swigging it right out of the bottle. Soon he'd be sleeping and snoring.

The day her daddy stopped snoring and kept sleeping she remained with his dead body and figured the quiet would take her, too. She lay there while he decayed, the stink from his skin rising in the air until the neighbors called someone to come take him away. They burnt him up, cheaper than burying him, but she had no way to get him because she didn't pay on time and they told her *the ashes were buried proper.*

His voice faded from the house, but she still searched for it in the air, in the wind, beating down men she ran across who weren't good as him, cursing women who still had their father, who still had a history with roots to suck something out of this planet. But now she had none, no nutrients, no father. Dad was the beacon for the voice of God. When she imagined the Almighty, it was the image of her father: white-bearded, proud and proper, sitting on a throne, wearing a majestic cloak. Now instead of God on the throne, Dad was a bloody Jesus on the cross, and his rotting body released odors in the air from where they punctured holes to crucify him.

Dad ascended to the heavens in those odors.

She usually avoided her mental health case manager from

the community team network, but with Daddy's ashes it was different. She'd asked her case manager every way which way to help her get Dad's ashes returned.

Each time they dragged her to a hospital they would ask:

"What are your treatment goals?"

"To be with my dad. Someone took him and burned him and has him and I need to get him back."

But the workers just put their pills in her body instead of giving her what she wanted, so she was stuck wondering about her dad's body going up in flames. Daddy has to be in a better state, because things are most brilliant when they go up in flames. Even the cardboard boxes that Maya watched burn in the fireplace. Orange and yellow spirits dancing in the fire.

You'll be graced with the Messiah child soon. God will place it in your womb.

The thought, like a radio voice, comforted her.

You walk amongst humans as mother of a new God.

She rubbed her stomach, flat for now. Her menses was finished but the next egg would be from the heavens. Joy would light her insides soon enough. Pregnant again, and this time it would keep.

You will be graced with his loving touch.

She put a handful of Skittles on her tongue. Her teeth cracked the shell to the important chewy insides. Saliva washed over her mouth and a rush of sweet joy shot to her brain.

But she was still hungry and needed to eat. The food pantry would feed her. She'd get herself a can of chicken noodle, the kind with the pull-off tab you don't need a can opener for, and drink it cold. And she needed to talk to Pastor Ron, because the scattered mix in her head was all tangled up, the way it happens, the way she'd been warned about by her case manager and community mental health workers who pushed their pills and their therapy. Sometimes their hospitals.

She grabbed the cloth bag, the one whose handle had dangled off creaky shopping carts, and knew if she hurried, she could catch Pastor. She would share her story of the Second Coming in exchange for some food. Just Mary sleeping in the stable. And maybe Father Ron would share his blessed seed, enter her again, in a blissful communion, and this time she'd keep the baby.

She said goodbye to the shadows and whispers of the house, snuck out the side door, and walked towards the church.

Each wooden telephone pole that rose from the ground as she walked by mocked her with memories of back when she had flexed her muscles, her brain and her brawn, and was training to be a line worker with Detroit Edison. She was the first woman on the crew, and she scaled up poles better and stronger than most of the men, digging her boots into the wood, carrying fifty extra pounds of equipment. She was born with muscles that wrapped around her body like armor; it helped her throw shot-put in high school and pole-vault thirteen feet high, winning second in states. It helped her learn how to work the power lines, tapping into the electric current, using her skills to bring electricity to others, and she got a paycheck with benefits in return.

But the days came when she started talking too much, saying and doing things she should not have, and Detroit Edison put her on leave and she couldn't work there anymore. Since then, she'd been stuck in and out of hospitals and in a house she couldn't pay the taxes on and going to the food pantry when she needed to.

Word of Faith stuck out like a golden oasis against the grey of the city.

Pastor Ron greeted her with his permanent smile. His bald head so shiny, his skin gleaming like a reflective pond. Without speaking, he walked her past the big looming wooden cross at the front of the room where the congregation gathered on Sundays. The cross was empty—they don't show Jesus on the cross in this church—why? *Because he's off the cross*, Pastor Ron explained. *He's not on there anymore. How can we show him when he ascended?* Instead, it was just a big brown piece of wood, a cross that anybody can get crucified on.

Pastor walked her downstairs to the food pantry while he texted someone on his phone. He flicked on the basement light and it flashed in a bright white, then flashed off, blinking on again, off again, the way it does, until it finally stayed on for good and revealed everything in the light.

Pastor opened the door to the food pantry closet. She walked in with her cloth bag in hand. He was quiet and observant as she picked through the lines of food. She took a can of chili beans, because she knows they last. She didn't see Sociable crackers but saw Triscuits; expired, but with crackers it doesn't matter. She grabbed three cans of chicken noodle and could hear Pastor Ron's breath, could feel his heartbeat, and knew he'd soon say *it's time to stop, you've taken enough.*

She started taking food faster, her hand wouldn't go as fast as her brain and she imagined all the places she wanted to go after Pastor Ron gave her a talk. She wished her thoughts would slow down and it felt like she needed a *man* because she's got the itch all inside her. Someone needed to give her their seed because she's the mother of a new angel and God would tell her if Pastor Ron is the one because he left it in her once but then forced her to take it out.

"Maya, I need a word with you. I don't think you'll need all of those."

He stopped her sooner than usual. There was still room in the bag for more food. She turned to look at him, standing in the doorway.

"You must already know," she said. "You know that I'll be with child soon. Anointed."

His smile was a space heater, his eyes the faucet of a warm shower her body needed. She left the pantry and went to the table where they'd sat so many times before. Where they'd spoken so many words and she sometimes took off her clothes and they found a place on the couch to unite. He always listened with his head at a slight tilt, a bow before a queen whose heritage had been denied, his fingers folded, as if her next sentence was the one he was waiting for. Always smooth shaven, like a baby boy who never grew a hair, never aged. His sermons came out in power on Sunday as loud and ferocious as his quiet stillness is now.

"Last time you were here, you spoke on some things.

Your speech was touched by God — speaking in tongues, they call it — but you get stuck there quite often."

"Sometimes it touches my tongue, sometimes my heart, soon it will be my womb."

He folded his hands and spoke out of his grin.

"But we've talked about how you should take *The Word* in acts of faith, and care for yourself."

Something was wrong. She could feel it. Pastor Ron's head started to quake, his fingers tightening in the fold in front of him, like he was about to choke something. She needed air. She needed to make the holy man feel what she was feeling.

"I know I've done some things people don't understand. I do them sometimes. But *you get me* though. That's why I come here. In this basement, a bit closer to the hells but learning about the heavens. You remember what we used to do down here? Remember? I know you do, we called out God's name together so loud. And then you took me to a hospital and they sucked it out of me. But we can try again."

"We do not talk about that, remember? You promised. It was like a bad dream, okay? But what is *not* a dream is what you did. The fight you had. That woman needed a doctor, and I heard about the words you spoke. They were hurtful. I can feel the unease within you still, and it needs to heal."

She looked down at her body. *It's not mine. I'm not in it.* She didn't care about the red nail marks that ran from her neck to her chest. She remembered the woman who made them and remembered the words she spoke. The volcano that erupted inside her.

"I fear you need some assistance with hearing God's message. There is a place you can go for this."

She recognized the tone of his voice. Goosebumps sprouted in her skin.

"I'm not going anywhere with you. I know what happens. I've seen it."

"These people are professionals. I have trust in them. They know how special you are, how strong you are. You've done things no human can. Your brain is so special. Amazing.

I've not heard anything like it."

Then she realized the shadows in the room, the ones she thought were just in her head the way they so often are — the things she's learned to ignore so she can concentrate on what's in front of her — the shadows turned into a person who was moving towards her from the corner.

And then the shape split into two white people, one big man, one tall white woman.

She clutched her canvas bag and she sprung to the air, jumped on top of the table, and towered above them. Pastor Ron looked up as if he'd seen the devil and was unprepared. The approaching people rushed forward but she swung the canvas bag full of canned goods at the man. He turned his back at the last minute, and the bag full of metal smashed into his back. He staggered, got his balance and came back again, but this time angry.

She readied for another swing, but he ducked his shoulder, grabbed her legs, and put her up over his back. She smashed her elbows at the back of his neck, her body was like darkest of coals and her heart a fiery boiler. She hated he could put his hands on her — the anointed mother of God. She could taste his scent, smell his secrets, and feel his sludgy white skin stained with dirty deeds. *He hasn't earned the right to touch me.* She didn't want him to catch whatever strand of God's gift she'd been blessed with.

Her legs kicked ferociously and Pastor Ron shouted out, "Calm down, we won't hurt you," but the chorus inside her roared louder than these devils who were trying to capture her and take her to their places. She had fight to give. Her arms thrashed with all *His* glory. Elbows, kicks, claws. She'd battled others before. She has a strength that sings with towering crescendos into notes unheard, and when it happens, she can flip over tables and burn down kingdoms.

She breaks free.

She saw her escape up the stairs and started to run, like Jesus ascending from Hell.

But Jesus never faced the syringe. The needle came out

like a silver serpent, puncturing her skin and she felt its old familiar contents — the Haldol, the Ativan — muscles mushy and melting. She was their puppet to command.

They carried her out. With each bounce her eyes drooped, rolling farther, farther, farther into the back of her head. For a moment she saw her insides, and she knew they couldn't be touched. They were trying to kill the child of God in her womb before it could be born.

They took her to their hospital and kept her brain in a fog, keeping her so confused she couldn't tell what day it was or what person she was.

And after some days in their building, the fog cleared and she was staring at the doctor lady, face-to-face.

7

MAYA IN DOCTOR ZITA'S OFFICE, 13 DAYS LATER

There's a look you get only from a hospital nurse. Maya could taste each glance, right on her tongue, sometimes bitter, sometimes sweet. They wrote notes about what they saw, how much she ate, if she went to their 'life skills' groups. There were so many people in this place, their thoughts and words just confused each other. Patients dressed in hospital clothes that sometimes looked like doctors, and doctors that sometimes looked like patients.

This hospital was a strange city.

The scratch marks on Maya's body had started to heal. The memories of her manic rage blended back in with the rest of her skin. Her thoughts slowed and became weighed down with depression and anhedonia.

Doctor Zita had called her into her office, just another person with a badge to mess with her life, that was nothing new. But this place, Northville Psychiatric Hospital, this vast compound, was new to her.

"Can you tell me who the president is?" Dr. Zita asked and then curved her lips into the warm hint of a smile.

"I can't name a single way any president has ever helped me. Naming one won't help."

She didn't know this doctor, and she wasn't about to get any closer.

"I want to know how aware you are, that is all, Maya. I've been observing you. I've seen you sitting against the walls. I've watched you scanning the room, not talking to anyone. Nurses tell me you were cheeking your medications on the first day, and since then you are refusing them entirely. We hope you see the benefit of them, but if not, that can't last."

"I feel your eyes on me. Always. Don't think I don't know when I sit in the day room and you walk by. And don't think I don't know you folks will start jabbing me with the needle if I don't start taking your pills."

"You're in control, Maya, or you can be. Just take ownership of your life and step up, use us to get what you need, and we won't have to use forced meds by injections."

"Might as well just jab me then," Maya said. She knew about forced meds. You don't take them by mouth, then they hold you down and they inject you with a needle. Some bitter nurses make them hurt. They want you to change your mind and agree.

"I appreciate your strength more than you can ever know, Maya. You are more special than others. I see that, I have lived with it. You will soon learn of my respect for you. We have a chance to do something special here if we make the next right move."

"You have no idea how amazing I am and what I can do. Right now I'm just tired. Tired."

"Oh, I do know what you can do. But do you? You need to know your own power." The doctor said her words as if by accident, as if the thoughts became too much and needed a way to leak out. The words squeaked in a different pitch, like air from a pinched balloon.

"Why am I in this place?" she asked. "Never been to this one, why not one of the others? You're too big here. This hospital is like one big jail or some weird-ass Noah's Ark. I don't like the smell of these people. They don't want to leave. They think this world is all there is, you keep them here with all your rooms but this little city just ain't right. Ain't right. Why am I not at Henry Ford Hospital or a place like that?"

"You've been to all of those lesser places, now you've reached the zenith. This building is state-of-the-art, unlike anything you've ever seen. Only problem is, we are closing. Not real soon, but soon enough, and trust me, you will stay here until we close. Stuck inside here, unless…"

"Unless what?"

"Unless you agree to be part of our transition program. There are systems in place for people like you who can move out sooner. You've been living hard. All your life, things have been hard, but you've grown brilliantly sharp because of it. An oyster. A diamond. I see the beauty and power in you. I'm here to make it grow."

This was a trick. Maya could hear the forked tongue.

"You're closing?"

"Yep, and you're here until the end…unless you agree to be in our transition program. There will be lots of benefits. For one, you know we have a pastor. He'll be here on Sunday, but I'll let you talk to one sooner, if you wish, if you…."

"I'm sure you got a pastor and a damn church, but I don't need to talk to a pastor. They say one thing, do another."

"I know about that, Maya. I know about the abortion. You pastor tried to hide that, but I know. He did tell me of your strength — in your body, your spirit, your perception. That's why I picked you. So many people trying to dull you down. Well, not here. I know you're special. We picked you. The power of your bipolar is a gift, a treasure that humans have lost, forgotten. You are an example. You see, I know about you."

"What do you know?"

"Well, for one, Pastor Ron said he was convinced you had read the obituary of every funeral he had done the last few months because you could recite their story… but you and I know that didn't happen. You didn't read the obituary, you heard from the dead, echoes of their words, because you pick up on these things, you can hear the subtle soundwaves that remain when for others the sounds are silent. At least when you're manic you do, but others say you're psychotic.

"And he told me of the strength in your body. Your senses, so astute others say you're insane. I know at Detroit Edison you made the mistake of telling them which zip codes had no power by the sensations on your flesh. If they would have checked, they'd have seen you were right, but instead they let you go. You've learned to keep quiet about these gifts because people hurt you for it, but you *don't need to lie to me*. I hope you hear the difference in my words."

"What is it that you even want? You're saying all this just

51

to make me take your drugs? Might as well tell it to the judge instead of wasting all your breath on me."

Doctor Zita felt her words of refusal, Maya thought. She could feel a change in the weather, and was hoping the doctor was ready to let her leave the office, but instead the doctor came back with her own lightning strike.

"You miss your father." The doctor leaned closer, a glint in her eyes. "You can hear him now, can't you? Or at least soon you will, when the mania returns."

Maya's heart stopped. Her lungs stopped. Everything froze in cybernetic stillness, all except her eyes, which traced the doctor's hand.

Doctor Zita had reached into her bottom desk drawer and pulled forth an urn. She placed the urn on the desk, closer to Maya than herself, as if presenting a gift.

"If you wish, you can take him out, spread him upon the table. These ashes could be from anywhere, that is true, but you can hear him more clearly now, and when your depression fades and your mania hits its peak, it will be even more clear. This is your father. I've brought him to you. You can bring him with you to the bipolar transition program. But if you refuse to go, I'll bury these ashes in a place you'll never find. Somewhere people are forgotten in a world you'll never know."

Maya could feel her dad's words; *You were left with me, Maya, but I didn't leave you.*

She grasped the chair handles, preparing to stand, to dash towards this doctor and demonstrate her might and give her a proper beating, but she paused at the brilliant glistening of the urn that spoke to her in voices she'd been waiting so long to hear. Moments later, she signed the paperwork to enter the transitionary program for Bipolar Disorder.

They took her down to the tunnels, pushed her on a stretcher, first along what looked like well-traveled routes, wide enough for a family to pass, but then down to the underground hallways. Her eyes traced the huge pipes that ran alongside the ceiling, transporting the heat and the water and whatever else they put into the patients here.

When they took a turn into a new passageway, the pipes stopped. The hallway became so skinny the stretcher bumped against the sides.

And then the final descent to her new room in the underground tunnels.

The man who pushed her seemed so big, so cold, like he was stuffing her inside an urn but forgot to burn her up first. This place felt like a crematorium, and they were ready to swing the door shut, and the fire was coming.

8

MAYA IN THE TUNNELS

"Maya, I will do my best to guide you on your journey. First, we will press you deep into yourself. We're preparing your body, getting it ready for the next cycle. Coiling, in a sense, so that when you spring back up it will turn you into something magnificent. For now, you're going to feel the depths of a new kind of depression."

The psychiatrist reached down to where Maya lay in the bed and put a hand on her cheek.

Psychiatrists don't do that, they rarely touch you, not tender, that's for sure.

The feel of the doctor's hand on her face stayed with her, even after she was left alone in the room. The area was dank, like a storage room with hospital equipment and cords and a bed in each corner. Nothing like in higher up floors where Maya roamed the hallways, looking out windows — windows made so nobody like her could jump to their death. She had gazed down at the houses below filled with people who didn't care, who wanted her locked up as they got into their cars and raced about the world.

This new room had no windows at all, just people coming in and out, and the doctor telling her how special she was — *as if I don't know* — making promises with that swindler voice of hers that Maya's been hearing for years.

But when she had brought the ashes…Maya felt the golden brilliance of her father chasing away the confusion in her head, the constant chitter-chattering thoughts like little icy men in her head chipping away had finally stopped, like the little men had dropped their tiny axes.

Was this all some trick?

No. This is no trick. You are the mother of a new race, a goddess. Your womb holds the salvation.

She would not have agreed without that sound of her

dad's voice. A voice that is more than a sound, it's a *color*, reflecting right off the sheer surface of Daddy's urn. When she was a little girl and he carried her on his shoulders, she could see the world on top of the giant. It made her feel big. When the neighborhood boys said words to her, Daddy sent her out with stronger words to say back. When teachers sent her home from school, he taught her things they could not.

You were left with me, Maya, but I didn't leave you.

The urn was now bedside, and she wondered what Dad thought about being here with her. The room had a lower ceiling with more humidity in the air. The moisture stuck to her skin and to the cement walls. It all felt sealed off, like a bunker, and she was all alone. Tiny red dots in the upper corners of the room blinked on and off.

Cameras. They were cameras, and they were watching, same way she felt eyes on her most of her life, but now at least they weren't pretending. Everybody was in on this. They had been all along.

They brought pills, the kind that dissolve on your tongue, and she took them willingly. Sometimes things got stuck into her veins — sharp syringes and cords stuck in her arm, tubes leading to bags of fluid, food came so rarely, she wasn't sure if she was being fed or eating her own insides.

She started to dry out. The voice of Dad's ashes went silent, like the last lyrics of a song, falling down a well, little echoes she wanted to reach down and grasp but could not, until soon she was alone, dry and lifeless.

The doctor was turning her to ash, letting her rot, the way she had always wished.

That's what this really was. Her tongue so parched she kept lapping at the roof of her mouth but found no relief. She needed to cry but her tear ducts were empty. She could feel them under her eyes, in her cheeks, just a dry, dusty well. The hospital machinery next to her watched the torture.

Air that smelled of chemicals came through the vents. Each new pill and each new visit by the doctor left her as the dying queen of an ant colony who could never spit out new life.

Her womb had been hallowed out like a pumpkin, all the best bits to grow the seed of the savior scraped out and discarded.

Her hands cupped between her legs, trying to warm anything inside a uterus that can't be saved.

What did they do with it after they took it out of my womb? They put it somewhere, the parts that were to sprout into Jesus surely miss me.

And why did they come for Dad's body and not mine?

She clenched her eyes shut tight as she could, squeezing them until the eyeballs inside squished. Everything inside her body was ready to ooze out and drain into Hell. She was disintegrating, slowly, like dad's body that faded to dust by such tiny degrees. The stench of his dying flesh released in the air and alerted neighbors.

Mom poisoned herself with pesticide. She got out of this life early, and Maya would do the same if she could. She would stab herself right into her heart, and her body would die and decompose until it stank enough that they would show mercy and burn her to ash.

Her black skin no longer felt like the rich garden soil but instead a rotting cadaver. Jesus harrowed Hell after he was crucified, looking for lost souls, and he needs to come back, because that's where she was, stuck in Hell with nobody to save her.

Day and night didn't matter in these depths. The faces of other patients she saw days earlier were just memories out of focus, all of them oblivious they were walking on her grave.

But then the moment came when she began to rise. It started with her eyes popping open after the drip, drip, drip of the IV bag beside her started to buzz. She felt like a Detroit Edison line worker again, connected to the electric grid of the city and to a magnificent surge of energy. She was a phoenix rising from the ashes in a flame of brilliance. Each boom of her heart shot blood of fire through her veins.

Maya was the Goddess she was meant to be, the mother of God. She heard the voices of angels, an army of midwives, ready to deliver the newborn king.

She couldn't stay still any longer and rose from her bed. Her womb was moist with life, fertile, a soil ready to receive seed.

The room became alive and vivid, the grey cement turned into a fluid rainbow, the prison became a garden. There was life inside. She wasn't alone—another beating heart in the corner. She pulled out the IV—maybe she wasn't supposed to do that, but she craved freedom. Blood seeped out the tiny IV hole in her wrist.

She put her arm to her mouth and tasted her blood. It made her shudder. Her dry tongue soaked it in, but she needed more, needed the fluid of life inside her body, in her mouth, in her womb.

God, she needed more.

In the corner, she saw him rising out of his bed as if summoned by the same force, muscles bulging, body shifting, strength inside in fluid motion.

They met in the center, not with a kiss, but with bodies pressed. His chest muscles pressed against her breasts. She buried her head into his shoulder and bit against his clavicle and tasted his skin. Her wetness was aching and longing and ready to receive. She pushed him down, and when his erection entered her, breath escaped from her lungs. The surge inside as if every atom was shifting.

She moved on top of him with ferocity, grinding her hips in unison to his thrust, moving him in and out of her and with each motion a new level of ecstasy. Rising heat turned the whole room a shade of vibrant red. Her hands pressed down on his chest so hard she thought he would embed in the cement, and if he were to stop now it would certainly be a new agony. She felt him sliding in and out of her wetness to a more glorious and savage heaven, getting so close to exploding. Moisture from her womb dripped and chilled against her thighs.

They were two snakes intertwined, eating each other, and then one snake, eating itself. Her hands wrapped around his neck, squeezing his jugular underneath. His blood was so warm and full of nutrients, her skin the soil that needed watering. Her nails sharpened like her senses, first squeezing around his neck as he flailed underneath, ready to burst. Her hands were no longer hers but the beast's inside, the howl that came from her mouth echoed in the dungeon as she dug her claws into his neck, through his flesh and into his veins.

And then he erupted, finally, not inside her with his seed but out of his jugular with a geyser spray of crimson blood onto the floor.

His body deflated. She wasn't done, but he was. He was losing power. No matter how much she grinded her hips in protest, he deflated inside her.

Everything cooled and he lay there, flaccid and lifeless, and she ran about the room, smashing against walls, leaping up to try and snatch the cameras. They were scared of her on the other side of the wall, she knew this, but they would not answer her pleas. She was stuck alone with the body. The first few moments, she tasted the warmth of his blood, but once the living blood cells within him died, she stopped drinking from him, and instead, lived with the dead body. She was good at that. It would rot and decompose, like her daddy, and they would come for it.

She didn't sleep, her muscles needed movement, so she moved about the room with her new strength trying to keep up with racing thoughts. She pleased herself with her fingers, she spoke to her father, she heard him praise her soul. She made plans and needed out. She would go to the Word of Faith to preach, spread her word like Pastor Ron could not and the congregation would realize her glory. She spoke to them now, sure they could hear her thoughts penetrating these walls.

For three days her mind raced around the room until a mist came in through the vents, this time not red, but a silver mist. She became lethargic, dazed, a punch-drunk boxer trying to stay in the fight. She finally fell to the ground, sadness and lead in her veins too much to carry. As the doors to the room opened, her eyelids fought the need to close. The dead man was dragged away. She was clothed with a robe, as if she were being prepared to be laid out in a wake. When they put the IV back into her vein and placed her on the bed, the doctor's palm touched her face once again.

Her skin was warm, comforting.

"You have to coil again, Maya, I'm so sorry, you have to go to deeper."

The chemicals made her dive back to depths of depression. The room turned to shades of black. Her father's ash started to stick together in the humidity, his voice impossible to hear. Instead it was the voice of her mother who summoned her.

I'm here for you my sweet child. Your dad doesn't know you like I do. You are me and you were supposed to join me. You need to get out of there. We can be together, you and me and all of us. Your child is here with me. They took her out of you and now she's with me. She was to be a girl but was killed before she could breathe on her own. That's what you and I do — we kill. You can't escape.

She remembered the abortion. The post-procedure pain in her womb, the emptiness. They put the child into medical waste, but she wished they would have given her the ashes. Pastor Ron told her she would be forgiven and the unborn infant would go straight to Heaven.

The memories taunted her in her depression, and she endured it all by cupping her womb.

Then the morning came when again she felt the new sensation in the IV and the red mist in the air. It tingled like cinnamon in her blood and made her body expand, new muscles surging, eyes sharper than before but sinking into her skull. She rose with mania to a new man in the room. This one seemed more powerful, and when he moved towards her, she lay on her back, spread her legs, and opened herself up.

Her hands scratched down his back as they fucked, each sharpened fingernail drawing blood. She could taste his plasma. She reached down to his backside and pulled him inside her, roaring into the heavens, thanking God for all creation. The pleasure surged through her spine, into her brain, out into her arms that could not help but reach up and tear at him. Her nails ripped one side of his cheek, then the other, then into his eyes and the side of his neck. He leaked blood on top of her, spreading his sticky warm blood onto her breasts.

Soon his carcass was laying on top of her, dead before their time to fully know each other.

Three more days without sleep, the blood of another dead man on her fingertips. Her body dashed about the room, just one tiny atom in a larger cell, spinning furiously, whirling into a tornado of energy that she was sure would lift her right through the roof into the glory above.

But instead, she was stuck, and after three days passed, they again used their chemicals and their silver mist.

"We have to coil you down again, so you can spring up higher."

God please abort me, scrape me from the womb of this dungeon.

She couldn't seem to die no matter how hard she tried, but soon again, she felt celestial beings pull at her heart and bring out the goddess, one of rage and desire, of wisdom and an insatiable urge for *more.*

Across the room, she saw another man, the third. He was tapped into the same drugs she was on, she was sure of it, and he rose from his bed just the same. His eyes looked her over, feasting on her. Her muscles contracted and flexed. Her bones wrenched and groaned, adjusting to the new strength, elongating along with her nails. Her teeth. Her senses.

She could hear things like never before. This man was lost and suffering, trapped here just like her.

She was going to tear into him like all the rest.

9

DRISCOE'S FIRST NIGHT IN THE TUNNELS

Driscoe's new bed was in a deeper place, somewhere well below the surface. The center of the earth was tugging at his chest and the world above him held more weight. Over the days, it seemed to crush his ribs under its mass, and if he listened close enough, he could hear his sternum cracking, like frozen ice. The walls around were no longer white, but grey cement, same as the inside of his skull— rough, ragged, lifeless. He opened his eyes and it felt the same as if they were closed.

A bed was in the opposite corner of his room with a body wrapped up in the covers like a mummy. A woman's black hair spilled on the pillow and a heart beat at the center. A living human was inside but just as empty and aching. White sheets seemed alive they moved so much, the limbs inside tossing and turning as if each new position will bring peace, but none does, so move into the next.

Others have lived here before. Their agony stuck to the walls and floated in the air. It mixed with his own and made a stew. Some even died here.

A port catheter was stuck in his chest. Machines hummed next to him, like the breath of an animal hibernating. He was wrapped in sheets, naked underneath them.

He heard footsteps and knew who was coming. The bearded man, wide body, clubs for arms that couldn't hang straight. He replaced the IV bag with something new, thwacked at the line with his fingers to make sure there was a steady stream into Peter's vein, then held out a pill.

Driscoe opened his mouth and accepted the offering. His tongue wouldn't make saliva but he was handed a cup of water to swallow, and the pill dissolved in his stomach.

It felt like his psyche was being operated on, but they forgot the anesthesia.

Wrapped tightly in a ball, just a fetus stuck in this cement womb, he cursed ever being born. Sleep and wake was indistinguishable, he wished his fingernails could claw into his veins, open them up and bleed right out.

"You're going to know a new kind of depression," Dr. Zita had warned him. "You've not felt this before, I promise, but you will rise to a higher state than you've ever been."

Something sinister slithered inside his veins. He stared at the liquid in the IV bag. The bag itself seemed a living being, like a jellyfish, floating in this cellar. It has a brand name, *Baxter*, written across, and he thinks of the Baxter factory workers who make these pieces of plastic. He sees them at work, their faces grin as they conspire against him. They know the pain they cause at Baxter, but one of them must have mercy. One of the bags has fluid that will come inside and stop his heart and give relief from this black ocean bottom he's fallen down to.

Instead he lives on. It's sinful to create a consciousness to suffer like this. The memory of seeing his daughter Kori in the monitor was burnt into his mind's eye.

Kori will be a star in the night sky that he will never see. She will travel to the places in the world people say you shouldn't. He hoped she remembered the guitar strings he strummed for her.

He remembered the mania that had built the days before *the incident*.

His mouth couldn't share the joy fast enough, the grandeur and splendor of things. The air was awhirl with his music. His senses were on fire picking up on scents unknown. He'd been awake for days, wanting and needing to *spread the word*.

The night he hurt Kori, he had grabbed her arm and nearly ripped it out of the socket, but it felt like the strongest bit of compassion, an urge he wished he'd resisted but instinct made that impossible. Grabbing her arm at that moment was full of love and urgency as if pulling her from a fire to save her life, to set her free.

I want you to hear the message. I need to pull you to safety.

The best of intentions, the worst of results.

The police were called. They hit him with the tasers, and all that did was enrage him further. Then the slug that burned into his shoulder from a gunshot, straight through and into the wall. Finally, he was cuffed. Three nights at the hospital, seventeen days in jail, and then living out of hotels, cleaning up for child custody hearings and swearing to the judge he would *get right.* A leave of absence from work, meeting with the union rep.

Time on his hands, and he wrote up history lesson plans — elaborate lessons that he then discarded days later for being too ambitious, nonsensical, the worst parts of him came out.

As the divorce played out the judge granted him limited visits with Kori, but it was clear she was scared of him unlike ever before. "Your veins were coming out your neck," she said. "You were so angry. I saw them shoot you, and it only made you more angry."

Last time he saw his wife in a famous final scene. He had just dropped Kori off and was standing on the front porch, like a salesman his wife wanted rid of. Her eyes looked down the street nervously as if a neighbor might see some secret exchange that shouldn't be happening. Whatever words she needed to say would be said outside — you don't invite monsters inside.

"You are loved," were his wife's last words on the front porch.

"You are loved," she repeated.

But she didn't say by whom.

He decided to leave his family and move on and never return. Sometimes he went too far and they put him back in the hospital. Other times, he stayed in hotels and lived on cocaine and meth and half pints of whiskey.

Now his new home was in this dark cellar, and it felt like the bottom of a grave.

Medical staff shuffled in and out. People were looking down upon him, *closed circuit TV monitoring*, there must be devils on the other side, come to see how humans would handle their hell. The depression was penance for leaving his family, and the ceiling above him held the weight of this world. The scent of suspicious gas hung like clouds near the ceiling.

"You made it, now it's time," the doctor said alongside his bed. She was the confident, crafty magician, who had just sawed his assistant in half and was about to sew him back together.

She injected something into his veins. Something full of cold electricity, and he detected a trace of cocaine. No, not cocaine, maybe crystal meth. Certainly some type of homemade amphetamine, but more pure, and his blood cells rushed to greet it, a long-lost vitamin meant to feed his plasma. Something longed for but never obtained, never thought possible until this day.

It filled his spine with such force, building pressure, compelling him to rise. Goosebumps spread upon each bit of his body, as if something beastly was trying to escape. Each muscle with building strength, forcing his bones to grow to keep pace. His erection raged with warmth, and he was propelled to the woman across the floor. She finally rose from her near-coma in the sheets, skin glistening, supple skin, sirens screaming in his ears. He was upon her and she greeted him with equal force.

They kissed as much as chewed upon each other's lips, both needing to taste each other. She was of his kind, that part was unspoken.

She clawed upon his neck, squeezing so tightly his jugular was closed shut, and his face burned hot. There was death on these fingers. He could feel the lives of those who died at her hands. They called upon Driscoe to join them.

His hands reached up to her neck and squeezed just as tightly, something ecstatic as they both danced near life and death. He entered her with a gasp, her body squeezing upon his erection as if trying to milk the life right out of him. Her nails tore at him, and his chest was getting ripped open by degrees, shards of skin peeling off like bits of beef jerky.

The orgasm was an explosion, and what he released into her seemed not of his body, but something siphoned from the center of the earth. He wasn't sure if he was dead or alive but was certain that he was forever changed.

10

MAYA IN THE TUNNELS

The itch had been unbearable, and her body rushed across the room to meet his. They had tangled and writhed on the floor, she squeezed his neck, he squeezed hers back. He had entered her with such immediacy she gulped air with all her might and sucked in all the colors and wonders of the galaxy into her lungs.

This one did not die like the others.

When it was over, she lay down on her back and wrapped her arms around her legs and pulled them into her chest. She then rocked back and forth. The movement felt instinctual, life affirming, and as she did, she felt the sperm burrowing inside her, and then fertilizing of her egg. The tiny seed of life secured onto her ovary walls. Impossible as it seemed to her, she felt all these things sure as one feels the caress of a finger or the rumble of her stomach.

She looked at her mate. His neck was already bruising in purples and reds, his skin gleamed savagely. He was bleeding from his chest as if he'd been ravaged by an animal but survived the attack.

"What was that?" he asked, still breathing hard. He looked at her as if unsure his words were human, but saw understanding in her eyes. "I've never felt anything like that — I've felt a lot of things, but never that. *What was that?*"

He wasn't going to wait for an answer, but rose from the ground. "I can't stop. I have to go. We're stuck in the apple orchard, aren't we?"

She lay on her back as his words buzzed about the room, his skin twitching, thoughts too fast to speak, blood coursing through their veins with such speed, some of it seeping out the cuts and scratches.

He started inspecting crevices in the room, looking closer at the cement walls, gazing into the video camera. His naked body paced back and forth like a tiger and she watched him as if he was a zoo animal. His eyes sunk into dark caverns, deeper by the moment, the colors swirling like a living, breathing cats-eye marble. Each muscle seemed alive and slithering under his skin, buttocks that reminded her of a prize race horse, quads flexing, ready to spring like a jungle cat, each muscle-clad arm a weapon, his skin glistening in the wetness of blood, of sex, of beauty. At times he stopped pacing to pound against the door without a handle, to scream for release towards the cameras to whatever entity was watching, then he turned inward.

He spoke not to her but to the walls. "Every spiritual truth is true. We know this. I know this now, I felt it inside you, but we can get out, *bust out*, if we just reach high enough."

But instead of reaching high, he dropped onto the ground, back muscles expanding as he did frantic push-ups. Next, he got to his feet, threw his hands to the floor, and did a handstand, both his feet high in the air, arms holding the full of his weight, gravity of the earth making his muscles expand like wings that looked so beautiful. He walked on his hands the length of one room, then back again, flipped back to his feet.

"It's circular, circular, circular insanity — making a new child when my first one about to get trapped by a Zita, but we never felt anything like that, right? You and I, up in here. A garden of a new Eden."

He stood back up and his words kept firing; "The only ones for me are the mad ones, mad to live, mad to die, desirous of everything at the same time," he said, walking in circles. "That's Kerouac," he pronounced, as if important. "We're just an advanced breed of monkeys on a minor planet of a very average star — but we can *understand the universe*. That makes us *very special*." He pointed a finger to the ceiling and declared, "That's Stephen Hawkings."

His words kept zip-zapping, and Maya knew he was a living, breathing, electric pole, and she was a special kind of line worker. She had lived all her life for this moment to know how to navigate that climb, to let the electric energy spark life inside her. She was a Doctor Frankenstein from the movies waiting for the lightning bolt to create life, and it finally struck.

"You're here with me, why?" he finally demanded she answer, sitting down next to her and gazing into her eyes.

"To conceive the Messiah," she said, not caring if he believed. "I have the ashes of my ancestor, and my brethren. You may think you were the father, but God was. You were just the vessel. God sent you here to survive me."

"None of us survive."

"Everything survives. Everything breathes, everything speaks, with a voice that fades but is never silenced," she said in contradiction, repeating words he had spoken before, but which she could still hear in this basement. Her body never felt so perfect, muscles around her womb so magnificent. Nothing could scrape this child from inside of her.

Dawn was breaking and she could sense the rising sun shining gold onto the forest outside. She felt the morning dew gathering on the foliage while birds chirped messages of hope. Rabbits moved under brush, hiding from the Hawks above, while deer in sets of three ran through the trees, sniffing with care, with vigilance, for there were predators about.

These hospital walls were in the middle of it all, and the two of them were trapped underneath the earth. A *cement garden of Eden*, he was right, he understood; he didn't know it, but he understood. Neither had any shame in being naked, her womb just petals of a flower, her breasts filling with the milk of life.

They had abandoned the beds for the cement floor which felt more natural and real.

Hours passed; the mania waned. The vibrancy of her body faded, the dip into depression fought off by holding each other. They strummed each other's limbs, rubbing with affection, feeling new sensations within their new selves. Their skin was covered in a mix of dried sweat, blood, and moisture from the cement walls. The hospital itself was sticking to them. The bedsheets in the corners of the room were stained, reminding her of who she was just weeks before, but now they both were something beyond human.

Maya felt her womb bustling with tiny bits of growth. She

was able to detect each new cell created, her own nourishment the life-blood for the child. They slept together naked, days at a time, spooning while both his hands wrapped around her growing womb as if it was the magical orb. Each day a metamorphosis. She felt something incarnate from inside him that wanted to protect her and protect the child, at all costs.

The room remained the same, but her eyes changed. The cement walls became a fibrous cocoon keeping her still, each camera on the wall a tiny red dot proving someone was watching on the other side. The IV drips had long ago fallen to the floor, but the air changed by the day. She could sense chemicals coming from the vents, seeping into her nostrils, into her lungs. Food was delivered on paper plates through a chute, and her mate galloped off to gather the fodder and bring it back to her. The meat was hardly cooked slabs of steak, and they ate without utensils, washing the meal down by a thick milk for breakfast, a sugary elixir for dinner. They shared a toilet that sat in the corner, no privacy, but each moment of relieving themselves no less natural than taking a breath.

When the last traces of mania had left and depression filled with every breath, they had less need for nourishment, and spent the moments embracing each other, taking turns in who was holding who. She didn't ask what brought him here, but she could tell they had similar reasons — terrible fear and wonderous hopes. She could hear his thoughts under that flowing mane of hair. He had no choice but to be here, like her, they were kindred souls.

She traced fingers along the curves of his arm, loving the sensation of her hardened nails against his skin. His beard had grown, his hair a lion's mane, her own flesh felt more like a hide than skin. Her breasts filled with milk faster than any woman of this world, her womb expanded just the same, the blessed manger for this miracle life. After just ten days, she started to show. His hand cupped her belly as if to test its size. He was no preacher. This baby would not get sucked out of her.

The infant was growing, and the new moon was coming. She could not see it in the sky, but could feel it the same way one can feel a sun beam on their cheek. A red mist was piped into the air, and they both soaked in the scents and felt its vigor.

"They're changing both of us more and more," he said. "They're making us what we only sometimes are, but making it stick. That's what they do in this room, and it's been done here before. We are not the first ones to be here."

He was right. She could smell the left-over scents of those who preceded their arrival, and inside each pheromone was the trauma of their memories.

"They plan to take this child," she said to him.

He looked back at her, pondering a world where your children are taken from you, and a world where a parent, a dad like himself, leaves his child Kori willingly.

"They take children from the mothers here," she continued. "I can feel their terror, it's still stuck to the walls like paint. I've had one scraped out of me. We can't let them hurt this one."

"You say *her*. You know the baby's a girl?"

"Yes, the next Messiah is female, and she won't be hurt."

"That's a lie. I feel a different truth," he said with a growl. "She will be hurt. It's inevitable. To be born is to be hurt. She'll come out crying, she'll live crying, she'll die crying and forsaken. And of all those who hurt her, you will hurt her most. You can't help it. It's what we do as parents. I did. I hurt my child. It felt like love at the time, but it turned to hurt."

He tried to get up, but the stickiness of their bodies forced him to peel himself off, like an amoeba splitting in two. He started to pace.

"I will not hurt her," she yelled back. "And you will not. Nobody can, you see, she can't be hurt. She won't be."

"Aye. You will. 'They fuck you up, your mom and dad, they do not mean to, but they do' — That's... that's... shit... who said that? See, I don't know anymore. I hate this. I should have been killed before I could make a child. I left my first before I hurt her more, and then they wanted to stick her inside a hospital like this. She has too much wonder, she doesn't need this bitterness. I know they lie when they say I might see her again. They lie about the promise, they don't lie about the threat."

"You will not let them take this child," she said. "I can feel it in you, I see it happening. You won't let them take her."

The depression that followed bought a sleep. The synapses in her brain lost its brilliance, their body lost the savage shine. The doctor coated them with a silver mist that sedated them into depression and felt like a leaden blanket. They were unable to stop them when hospital staff came in through the locked doors and injected their veins as they were wrapped inside each other's arms.

"One more time," they said as they shot up their veins. "After this, you two will cycle on your own. You've both done brilliantly."

The words were barely heard, the footsteps of the doctor leaving the room a far-off sound heard in the deepest dream, but as the moon rose outside the walls, and the energy came and red mist billowed inside the room, they felt carnal again. The meat they were brought in was completely uncooked. Neither of them felt any shame eating it raw with sharpened canine teeth and fingernails like steak knives. Juice dripped from their chins to their breast.

The mania made them think and move and collide, his energy feeding hers, neurons firing in his brain, valves of his heart opening and closing in rapid succession. His whole body changed with the mania, his face more primitive. He moved as a hunter, and her body and soul morphed into huntress and seer.

The history of what had happened inside the room was also rising and could be read loud and clear. Children were born here in anguish. Mothers woke from the stupor of the silver mist and then cried out when their offspring was missing.

"There are children in a room nearby," Maya told him. "They're close. They took the children from the patients who were here before us. They chained them up. They took their plasma, and they're injecting *that very plasma into us*. You know this is true, and you know you must protect her. They *are* going to take our child after she is born. You can't let them."

When the mania again faded, they returned to sleep on the ground, like a litter, finding warmth in each other's flesh and affection. They were naked and natural and fusing together in spirit. Weeks that followed, she could feel the stirring in her womb, and it was when the mania rose in her mood that her water broke, pulled from her as the moon pulls the tide. She felt herself transforming from insect to butterfly during the childbirth. The pain and glory of the birth brought noises from her mouth in decibels and howls like Saint Peter blowing his horn to announce *the Coming*.

The baby was covered in the fluid of life. Holy fluid. It soaked both child and mother as he cut the umbilical cord with his fingers and she brought the infant to her breast to feed. It fed from her body, but they were still one. She felt the ashes of her father beam with pride.

11

DRISCOE THE FATHER

The infant had not cried at birth, but the mother had announced her coming with a blast from her lungs that cracked his ear drums. The room had a raw scent, new to the world, covering them in a cosmic cloud to water a new kind of life.

The red lights on each camera in the ceiling corners grew a more eager shade of red, the eyes of the snakes watching, ready to strike. This was not the first time authorities here witnessed the birth of a child only to snatch them up shortly after. She was right about that.

Like his mate, Driscoe felt them too—patients who had been here before, giving birth in this same location to wailing infants who were then taken. The children were somewhere nearby, in another room, perhaps, but none of them as magnificent as the wonder who was feeding at Maya's breast.

Over her fifty-eight days of pregnancy, he'd been touching Maya's stomach as if transmitting messages through the tiny curl of her belly button, through her umbilical cord, straight to the beating heart of the fetus. The child was now breathing on its own, sparkling with life, a new-order being.

The infant's skin was translucent, the veins inside lit up like a Christmas tree. He could see inside the brain, like stars in a galaxy, neurons in red and orange lighting up as she suckled on her mother's breasts and gazed up at its benefactor, its cheeks pursing, and with every swallow it seemed to grow in microscopic degrees.

Another child. Another girl. He should not have been allowed to conceive again, to create another human and force her to face misery. Maya was right, he had to stop her from being taken. He would not let another one of his children experience pain and suffering.

"You see, she is anointed in ancient oils," Maya said.

"You planted the seed, but you are not the father, only the vessel, you are only here to protect her."

The more his mate spoke, the more truth became clear. They were being watched by cold-beings, devious doctors, and he would make sure not to fall prey to their scheme, make sure that this special child would not face whatever hurt they had in mind. There is no greater sin than to create a consciousness only to let it suffer.

He pictured Kori standing in the hospital lobby. If he could have reached through Doctor Zita's computer, wrapped his hands around the child, and brought her through the screen, both of them could have slipped into an eternal sleep, hand in hand, one permanent midnight. *Who said that? Someone said that*, that's what he wanted — one final permanent midnight with him and his child and they would suffer no longer.

But it was too late. He may never see Kori again, but not too late for this child.

All three of them spent days laying together, his mate upon his chest, the child feeding, always feeding, soaking in the mother's milk which seemed from springs eternal. The Mother's skin such a rich shade of brown, fresh soil, that sprang forth this baby with a skin tone never before seen. In the days that followed, the translucent flesh turned into a delicate armor, her cranium closed to cover a brain firing faster than any ten-day old ever conceived. The eyes of the infant had changed from the cold blue to reds and then oranges and yellows.

They ate raw meat and fed the child milk. They slept on concrete in one ball of flesh covered in the fluid of sex and birth.

"Truth is beauty, beauty truth — that's Yeats who said that, and that's bullshit. Truth is savage, bloody, dripping, primal — truth is you laying there, a queen."

"We don't have much time, be ready."

They would not take a child if the child were dead.

"The chemicals change us. The full moon and red mist lifts us up, and the silver mist puts us down. This has been their play all along."

"They don't understand us. We are eternal, they are

temporal."

Doctor Zita was the invisible deity watching over them. The heartless God was watching, the puppet master who controlled it all. But he would cut the strings, cut out their hearts and eat them while they were still beating if he needed to. He would do anything to make sure his child did not suffer.

They won't have this child. I will kill it first. I would do it a favor. Sacrifice a child as God would want.

They lay tangled in joy and sadness for days, but when the rush of mania started to build his instinct rose from his gut.

There is not much time.

The doctor and people in the other room were going to act. Driscoe waited for his mind to transform, for his muscles to pulse with energy, for his nails to turn to knives, his canines to sharpen, for the flaccid to become fierce.

With Maya feeding the infant, and him to her blind-side, he acted.

He snatched the infant fast as a cobra strike from her breast. She moved to stop him, but he had anticipated each twist of her muscle, and pulled the child from her grasp.

The infant was in his arms, and he dashed to the corner with his back towards the room, protecting his prey. His mate cried out in horror, just an echo of the many mothers who had also screamed inside this room. The terrible sound wouldn't stop him, this sacrifice was necessary.

With thumbs on the newborns throat and hands wrapped around her neck, he started to choke the infant. The child's eyes bulged in response, but she did not cry. She only looked back at him as if she knew what was happening, as if she had anticipated this moment.

There was awareness and wisdom in those eyes.

He needed to snuff that out.

The more the red and orange eyes stared back, the harder Driscoe squeezed.

Stop looking at me, don't see me like this.

Her nose had grown slightly wolfen, snouts for nostrils, eyes deep into her skull. Her skin felt like a smooth leather, and its neck muscles fought against his raging fingers.

But those eyes — like the red blip of the cameras on the walls, they looked into him and were recording the memory of this moment.

His mate was finally upon him and her claws ripped against his skin, shredding flesh and muscle. The pain brought a rush of such warmth to his muscles. The sweet sting of an opioid high.

Before she could attack again, the door to the cement room opened, humans from the other side rushed in, unprepared, frantic. Driscoe felt their confusion, their urgency.

His mate was caught in the middle, and she began flexing her muscles, arms cocked ready to strike, legs in fighting stance.

Not much time. Finish the job. Squeeze.

The light in the child's eyes were finally out, its neck was drooping. Its skin grown cold. The blood no longer rushing.

No more suffering, that was it.

He held the lifeless child in the air as if to present a gift to Doctor Zita.

Here. See, this is what I do. I hurt children. I'm not so special after all.

The doctor was armed with a gun, not full of bullets, but loaded with the leaden substance that they had been pumping into the air. Driscoe sensed it in the tranquilizer dart, and when the fired dart hit him in the shoulder, he immediately felt lead in his veins. It confused and slowed his thoughts and made him drop to the floor, looking up at her tall, lanky body.

The doctor scooped up the lifeless infant. In one arm she held the child, in the other, the gun. The child's mother nearby with such rage and passion that she finally let loose. She swiped at the doctor, her nails like talons, and ripped open the doctor's arm that held the child, shredding it as if in a tree chipper, dissecting muscles and ligaments. The child immediately fell from her grasp to the floor.

With one swoop, the big man dressed in scrubs grabbed the infant and dashed out the door.

The doctor stood between Maya and the exit. Her

tranquilizer gun was empty, but instead, she held a syringe, wielding it like a sword, trying to stab Maya as the infant was taken farther away.

Maya hesitated, surely sensing the deadening chemicals inside, and when the doctor tried to strike, Maya moved swiftly to the side, the doctor left helpless in surprise at her agility.

She can smell your thoughts, senses them, don't you realize what you made?

Driscoe's senses deadened further, fading into black. The last image he saw was Maya unleashing all her rage onto the doctor, slashing and tearing into her while she curled into a ball, protecting her vital organs. Maya then ran out the still open door, escaping the room, and leaving Driscoe behind.

The howl she wailed as she ran to save her child still makes his ears ring, the haunting sound of a soul on fire.

#

He'd always known that everything breathes, everything speaks, with a voice that fades but never silenced. Now he realized this knowledge was a curse, because he heard the voices that he wished were silent. Truths he'd rather not believe.

Maya would not find the infant.

The child had started breathing again under the doctors' care. Alive and at her will, she was taken and hidden into rooms unreachable. Maya had killed half a dozen humans on different wings of the hospital, busting through floors, searching for her baby while psychotic patients questioned their visions. Hospital staff scurried about helpless, relieved that the unbreakable windows were suddenly breakable when Maya finally jumped through them, six floors up, and landed on her feet. She ran into the woods as the full moon shined down like a spotlight.

She was gone, but her presence remained. Driscoe could feel her anger from the betrayal as if her spirit was still there, and his mania would not let him forget. It taunted him. Persecuted him.

After his mania came the depression, and then the tears.

Driscoe cocooned in his own depression for weeks, stuck in the cement loneliness, basking in his failures for weeks at a time. When the mania hit and his brain transformed, he growled in pain, at times clawing at his own skin to feel the rush and for relief from the hurt.

All alone, but next door, the chains kept clinking and clinking and clinking. The infants of previous births who were taken from this room were growing, getting bigger, stuck in the torture of their own suffering. They spoke to him. Whispered to him. Begged him to help. To feed them. They spoke with hurt that no human language could grasp.

The months passed and the hospital was indeed closing. The building above Driscoe was being emptied. The hospital was in transition. The weight was being lifted, patients moved to other places, the cacophony of voices fading by degrees, less staff, less equipment, *impossible to move it all, we'll have to leave the unnecessary parts behind*. The parts that remain will just fall to the floor like ocean sediment, discarded waste, just part of the rubble.

They were going to leave him there.

And as empty as his gut felt, he knew he would never starve, whatever they did to his body, it endured and lived on.

The agonizing quiet of his eternal tomb was broken when he awoke from a coma-like depression to find the door ajar. The electric locks had given way when the last bit of electricity was shut off, and he was free.

When Driscoe took his first steps out of his room, he didn't go to find Kori, he didn't go find Maya. Instead, he went next door to the beasts chained to the wall. They looked at him with the love that he used to get from his own daughter, but these were children he knew he could take care of. Children he knew how to feed. They offered him complete adoration as long as he fed them.

And chained to the wall, they had no choice.

Most had limbs with deformities, like an elbow joint that bent the wrong way, or an extra limb with no hand at the end. Some had teeth that made their mouth impossible to close. One was cursed with an eye that never blinked but instead was stuck open—always open. Their chains clinked together like murderous wind chimes when they moved.

Like him, they curled into depression when the time came, and then become savage with mania when the moon rose and summoned them to hunt.

As they grew, the chains got tighter around their necks. They squealed and squealed for food, and feeding them was his penance. He had deemed himself their father.

And he had *mouths to feed.*

12

2002 — PASTOR RON, SUNDAY, 10:42 AM, WORD OF FAITH CHURCH

Pastor Ron hit the light switch, and the cheap fluorescent tube clicked on and off, on and off, struggling to light up the basement, cycling in light and darkness, until finally, the room lit up completely and the darkness went away.

Pastor Ron was walking behind Trudy, watching her skirt bounce with each step. He had seen this same skirt more than once lift up in the wind on her Sunday morning walk into service, and he always imagined what lay underneath. A silk blouse hugged her breasts. Each curl of her hair tempted like a whispering snake.

"I'm sorry I have to ask for this," she said, "I never thought I'd need a food pantry before. You've done so much already."

"Food will nourish your soul and comfort your heart during these times of grief. I want to aid you in any way that I can. 'Come to Me, all you who labor and are heavy laden,' God said, 'and I will give you rest.' That is what I pray for you, Trudy, to take away your labors and heavy burdens."

"Those words you spoke at his service. They were so kind, so uplifting."

"Your husband was a fine man, and now you are missing something that all women should have. Your loneliness as a widow is a terrible burden."

"I still see him when I close my eyes. I don't really sleep. I just dream. In my dreams he's there. Next to me."

Trudy looked to her side, to the place where her husband might have been standing had he been alive.

"Your bed is empty, you're sad and alone. God does not wish this for anyone."

Trudy's body softened. She looked toward the food pantry, her legs nearly moving in that direction as well, but then

Pastor Ron tilted his head and flashed a smile and she froze in place.

Nearly ready to put her under his spell.

Parishioners felt so important when he offered up his devoted attention. Crowds might gather around him after he raised the roof with a Sunday sermon, but it was in these small deeds, these private one-on-one moments, that he really shined.

"Trudy, God made us in his image to care for each other. What are we here for, if not to heal each other's wounds? *'Blessed are those who mourn, for they shall be comforted.'* These words are not true because Jesus spoke them, Jesus spoke them because they are true."

He reached out and put a hand on her shoulder. It only took a slight nudge and she slid into a hug, engulfed in his arms, and he pulled her in tightly as he could. He could feel her heaving in soft tears.

"This is what God wants, to ease your burdens. The Lord is near those who have a broken heart."

He began rubbing her back, pressing her trembling body into his. He felt that unmistakable change in the weather, that detectable shift, the rhythm circulating into her body. He knew she was his to do with as he pleased.

He pulled her breasts against his chest, his erection rising. He bent down to smell her hair, his lips near the flesh of her neck, not yet a kiss, just his warm breath on her skin.

He led her to one of the donated couches that lined the basement walls, guiding her body as if she were dizzy and delirious. She was fragile and ready to crack. He knew he needed to do this now before she thought about what was happening.

His pulse pounded. He remembered the premarital counseling sessions he had with her just a few years earlier, asking her about getting married early, convincing her to hold his hand as they talked, his eyes on her body most of the time. Then the grief counseling the week of the funeral. She was a mess then, and he had offered words of hope. *It's not your fault that your husband died so young, he was a good man, but maybe not healthy enough for you,* and with each word she looked at him more as a Godly father. Groomed for this moment.

"Trudy, this is love. God would want this."

Her blouse unbuttoned, the brown skin under white bra so supple, her breasts revealed, and his hands upon them, then laying back on the couch and pulling her onto him, sliding off her skirt, his hands over her bottom. She was on top of him, as if this was her idea.

"We are meant to love each other. God is love."

Yes, this was heavenly. He looked into her eyes, rolling into the back of her head, the tears she was crying just evidence of healing. She looked away when their eyes met.

Why is she afraid to look at me?

It mattered not. He will make her feel relief. He entered her and…

Footsteps coming.

Not the first time he would be caught, and he would soon have to stop. The ensuing discussion of excuses flashed through his mind — *It happens in grief, Trudy, it's okay, you were overcome. God forgives us for all we do during times of such loss. We forgive ourselves and move on.*

He heard the steps dash towards him and he should have stopped fucking her but he was almost finished, in and out of her and ready to explode, but before he could Trudy was lifted in the air. Snatched right off his erection, like a crane, something had grabbed her neck and placed her elsewhere. Trudy gasped in surprise, followed by the roar from a devil who seemed to have risen right through the basement floor from Hell below.

A beast was upon him. Sinewy muscles flexing in power. Her hair both savage and noble waterfalling down the sides of her face, her eyes sunken into caverns, orange swirling pupils drilled into him with anger and rage. Her nostrils flaring. Mouth dripping with saliva off those lips… *those lips*. Those same lips he used to kiss. Her canine teeth were sharp and eager to be satisfied.

"What's wrong, Ronald? Don't you remember me?"

He did. This was Maya, or something that used to be Maya, and she had him pinned down on the couch.

"You fucked me here on this same spot," she said, and then swiped his face with her claws, ripping open his skin, four bloody slices across his face.

"You whispered words of deception in my ear to make me succumb," she said, swiping with her other hand, four more slices. With the sharp sting of each cut, more blood flowed down his face.

"And in my sickness, you tricked me into a hospital. And the things they did to me in there. The things they did... the torture. You banished me to Hell, and *another* child. They took her, too. Do you know what that feels like?"

She opened wide and revealed a mouth turned savage. Strings of saliva connected her deep lips.

"This woman is crying, grieving her soul-mate. She will blame herself, and you feed off her like a parasite. You know nothing of God. You are blind."

With that last word, she poked one finger straight into his eye, faster than he could blink. The pupil squished and pain shot through his body, every muscle flailing, but she matched his struggles with more might. She had one hand pressed against his chest and his fist banged at her to break free. His face bleeding, his eye blinded. He was helpless as an insect, about to be crushed.

God, he kept crying out in his head, *God, please help me...God!*

Sunday service. It's starting soon. His congregation would come. They would save him. Trudy would get help.

"And in my sickness, you convinced me to abort. They went into my womb and took out what you put inside me. Tell me, would you like to know what that is like?"

While she straddled his chest, she reached one hand behind her and her sharpened nails closed around his testicles. He howled in pain when she squeezed them in her palm and clawed into the wrinkled skin of his scrotum. Like the jaws of a shark, her nails tore into the skin, stretching and ripping, twisting and yanking, slicing with her nails, until finally, his scrotum released from his body. His whole groin was soaked in the blood of a thousand menses.

She held the bloody bits in the air as he screamed in pain. His mouth was open as wide as it could to let the agony escape, but the noise was soon silenced when she plunged a mouthful of his own testicles full of blood and semen inside his mouth. His airway was blocked, his tongue repulsing at the taste.

With both hands she covered his face, not letting him breathe, riding him as he buckled to get her off. He tried to swallow to get some air, to free his passageway and breathe.

It took 164 seconds for him to choke on his own testicles.

Before she left, she plunged one hand into his chest cavity towards his heart and gripped the piece of muscle, no longer beating, and she carried it up the stairs to the Sunday service.

13

Maya at Church

The smell of his blood coated her nostrils. Her palms were moist and sticky while she carried his heart, just a bit of tough muscle, in her hands. Strings of veins dangled and dripped, leading a trail up the stairs, through the foyer, to the chapel.

Her rage was not quenched, but it grew inwards with introspection.

This church had been a second home at times. A humble oasis enclosed by fading brick on the outside, while inside it offered an escape from the blight, one of many local urban churches dotted down these streets. It fit at least 200 members if you counted those who stood on the side during crowded Sundays. Flowers lined the walls, the lights flickered, made to look like candles, but one spotlight always illuminated the brown cross at the front of the room.

The congregation was gathering and they gazed up at Maya in disbelief. Some immediately made their way to the exit in fear, others remained, realizing this was an epiphany, a message of the majesty and splendor of God. A visit from Mary who'd given birth in a concrete manger. Their Sunday floral dresses swayed, suitcoats trembled, their faces full of inexpressible emotions under too thick makeup meant to impress, beneath it a mix of praise and sickness.

She stood before them, naked before the crowd, unashamed and unabashed, and she howled her own song of praise, stopping their breath for just a moment, taking them somewhere they have never been, no human has, with a song unheard. When the shock ended, the fear rushed in and they all started to vacate in fear.

Maya stood before the dark brown cross at front and held the heart outward as if in offering. This is your false god, your idol. At least twelve women in the crowd had succumbed to the whisper of the snake, their pastor.

The night before she had rushed out of the Northville Psychiatric Hospital basement with bezerker rage, manic energy, fueled by the pain of all those patients inside and having her daughter ripped from her grasp. She searched for her daughter in every level she could, but her daughter was hidden. She could not find a trace, and as her rage built, she busted out of the hospital altogether and landed outside on her feet ready to spring forward into the night.

Instinct helped her hide in the shadows of the city and travel barely detected, just a quick glimpse from humans who did a double-take; *Did you see that deer, or coyote, or...what was that?* Visible for an instant, then gone. She stayed hidden in the brush, behind a building, or she latched her nails, sharp as hooks, upon wooden utility poles and climbed the heights, riding the electric grid. Detroit Edison couldn't stop her. A line worker at last. The buzzing wires became part of her veins, her brain chemistry zapping with the power of the city. The electric current only carried her faster, scurrying to the object of her rage.

Now, standing before the panicking congregation, *she* was head of the church. Her howls filled the air. She held the pastor's heart, enough blood still dripping from it to fill a communion cup. She screeched with all the rage of a mother's hurt — every mothers' hurt from the beginning of time — echoing inside the Word of Faith.

The crowd rushed out, and she sensed forces closing in. Authorities had been called.

She left the heart as a gift, crucified and bloody, and bounded out the doors, down Grand River Avenue, to her home street.

Her childhood home stood tall and resilient, boards nailed on to cover the wounds. She pulled back the loose board and stepped back into her lair as if for the first time. It welcomed her, spoke to her, missed her. The scent of her deceased dad was fresh and sharp, the scent of his whiskey, just a waif, and the jingling of the ice cubes inside. She could still smell the cinnamon toast he used to make each morning. She could still hear the sound of his snores, like a lion's roar.

She'd been in the house with confused brain before, overwhelming stimulus coming from floating bits of dust, but nothing like this. She moved about each room and could hear each spider spinning their webs and taste the sound of each wooden creek. She bounded up the stairs to her bedroom as a girl, last door on the left, memories of playing alone on the floor with second-hand Barbies, white Barbies, but stained and dirty, like her, the way she felt. She'd been born so dirty, her mom had to kill herself.

But now so powerful. She wanted to rip the walls down, wanted to sing her song of rage and praise. She punched out the window and the shattered glass cut into her hand. The pain just made her burn more brightly. She stepped out onto the roof and the night air of the city greeted her eagerly.

The night was fresh and full of life and she smelled the beauty of the dark night, scents hidden to most humans, so rich and delicious. Her mate was out there, still locked in the hospital tunnels. Why didn't she act earlier when he snatched her child? As soon as he was upon her, she could feel his intentions — *the best of intentions, the worst of results*, but she was too late.

He wanted to save his daughter from being taken in the only way he knew how, by any means necessary, and for him, that meant to kill her.

She would find her daughter.

The image of the doctor was what she saw when her eyes closed. Her long legs, skinny body, deceptive eyes. Maya longed to rip her apart like a wishbone. Everyone whoever made her promises; doctors and social workers, teachers and therapists, Detroit Edison managers. They all let her down, took all she had, and left her alone.

She gazed over the city trying to detect the heart of her child, still out there beating. The dreams and fears, prayers of the humans on her block, invaded her senses with each breath, but no trace of her newborn. The moon was starting to sliver, the yellow arc a scythe ready to slice, the shape of an eye closing, watching down. The last bit of glow made her blood vibrate with energy. It hummed as much as any electric grid in this city.

The moon fell below the horizon. Birds started to chirp and scatter in their morning routines. Maya's power started to fade. Her muscles returned to their pre-manic state, her face transforming back to human. Exhaustion followed, as if each organ was shutting down, cocooning. She climbed off the rooftop, through the windowsill inside. She found a corner where the spiders lived and curled up nearby. She rolled her body into a ball and fell asleep as the sun started to rise.

She felt like a mass of dead meat when she woke, an unbearable heaviness that she hoped a shower would wash off her. Cuts and bruises all over started to hurt, not sure where she got each one, as her body returned to something familiar. In the bathroom, she looked at her naked self in the mirror. She traced a fingertip along her shoulder, down her arm. These arms had thrown shot-put in high school. These legs could sprint and jump, but nothing like the strength in body, mind and spirit she had just experienced.

Only deep sadness remained.

She turned the faucet on, *good, water still running,* even if the electricity and gas was shut off months ago. The cold water made her feel dead inside, as if showering in embalming fluid, and when she dressed herself, as if preparing a cadaver. She gathered a dollar and eighty-five cents in nickels and dimes, and went out into the daylight.

The sun attacked her with its brightness as she walked the streets. Scolding her, beating her down. Gone was the sweetness of the moonlight, instead the fiery coals of a scorching star. She never knew the daylight could be so violent.

She approached Owl's Party Store. The men were still there, leaning up against the side of the building, drinking beers out of wrinkled brown bags, their skin a deeper shade of brown but just as wrinkly.

She walked by them as if unseen, greeted by the ding of the bell announcing a visitor, and walked to the freezer. She had enough money for one pop, and got a Dr. Pepper.

"You notice I've been gone?" she asked at the counter. He

took her change and didn't respond, just put the coins in the register. She eyed the wicker basket of one-shot liquor bottles, wondering if she might steal a shooter of whiskey without him noticing, since he couldn't seem to see anything else.

"Want to know where I been?" she asked again.

He didn't answer.

She eyed a butane skull lighter, and wondered if it would even flame on for her if she tried.

She caught the change in her hand and walked out the store. She twisted the red cap of the pop and tossed it toward the open garbage where it bounced on the rim, once, twice, nearly falling inside, then fell to the ground.

Missed, but she wasn't picking it up, and moved on.

The carbonated water fizzed down her throat, mixing in with all the meat she'd been eating, filling her up with sugar and caffeine, but it wasn't enough. She still felt empty and drained. She should have gotten coffee and some Hostess donuts.

She stepped over each crack of the sidewalk, remembering her days as a child. It didn't matter if she stepped on a crack, she already broke her mom just by being born.

Mom, I wish I was with you. Look what they've done to me here.

She thought of doing what Mom did and ending her own life, but the energy it took seemed too much. Plus, if she tried and failed, she would only have her body, still alive and suffering, scooped back up and stuck in another hospital. Trapped inside again.

She found herself drawn to the church.

Each wooden utility pole that rose from the ground along the sidewalk reminded her of who she was just days before. All that was over, and her child was gone. Her mouth wouldn't make saliva so she guzzled down the Dr. Pepper. The liquid sloshed in her belly, and then soaked into her skin immediately, leaving her dry and lifeless. She drank more until the bottle was empty.

Cars filled the church parking lot, but this was no Sunday service, this was a Saturday funeral. People dressed in black walked somberly with heads down, heels and shiny shoes clicking on the pavement. A little boy wore a red tie and held his sister's hand. He seemed the only one who noticed her approach. He'd seen her just days earlier, holding the preacher's bloody heart in her palms, and she waited for him to point her out—*It was her! She did it! It was her!* But he did not, nor did others. Women in dresses kept moving on, each one trying to look better than the other. They wore black to show their respect for the dead, but they left their breasts exposed to get attention from the living.

She walked invisible through the parking lot, the stains from the pastor's blood still on her hands. The organ music greeted her when she entered the church. It used to make her feel alive and elevate her heart, but at that moment felt like opening up an unplugged refrigerator with moldy food inside. No longer could she smell every spirit, the glorious ones, the rotting ones. Instead it was all bland.

She wasn't a recognizable killer, just slightly out of place in her black tank top, jeans, and sandals. Sandals she had walked in so long the cork on the bottom was an imprint of her foot.

Someone offered her a seat but seemed upset when she took up the offer, just one of many here to watch the funeral.

Pastor Ron's funeral.

Nobody recognized her as the one who tore his genitals off, stuffed them down his throat, and then ripped his sick heart out of his chest and presented it to the congregation. *This is your king, and he's not a saint but a serpent.*

They gave his eulogy at the front, pacing back and forth in front of the looming brown cross, a cross even more empty than before, if that was possible. The cross seemed to grow from the ground, planted like a tree, and the speakers preached of Pastor Ron's dedication and inspiration. How he could anoint you with blessings like nobody on this earth, and God saw this and reached out and took him to Heaven to care for all our loved ones who died before their time. God takes the good ones first.

The crowd answered in signs of affirmation, raising their hands in deference, some moving to the beat of the speech.

Whatever evil it was that killed the pastor had only made the church stronger, the eulogy concluded.

Maya felt herself getting dizzy, head-spinning. Her gut swirled with soda and nausea. With a turn of her head she could see the woman who had lay with Pastor Ron in the basement when she attacked. And there were at least a dozen or more, most of them married, who the pastor had fucked. Maya hated that word, *fuck*, but that was the only one that fit.

Now Pastor Ron sat on the right hand of the father. Move over, Jesus.

When it was over, Maya heard the politicking of people murmuring about who would be the next lead preacher, trying to hide their own personal favorites under their breath. She got up wishing this had been her funeral, that she had been in that casket, and revered with the same passion.

In the parking lot, she walked with her head down. Nobody noticed she was alive, except one person, who cut off her path. Soon she was standing face to face with a tall white woman, briefcase in her hand as if delivering something important, and bandages all over her body. Bruises in red and purple peeked out the sides of the bandages, a hint of the wounds underneath, and one of her arms was in a sling.

"I thought you would come here."

It was Doctor Zita.

Maya's anger stirred so deep, but she was frozen inside. She wanted the coldness to thaw, or better yet, crack open, so she could reach up a hand to strike this woman, this doctor who beguiled her. But instead all she could manage was to make a fist and then turn her anger inwards. The fact that Doctor Zita was stitched up in so many places where Maya had scratched and clawed gave little solace.

"I know it was you who killed the pastor," the doctor said. "Maybe you should have. Maybe it was right. But now look at you? You are plain again and you made the man a martyr. You should have stayed in the hospital. The baby girl was going to be cared for. She's not yours. *We* made her. *I made her*. I made you, and I can take away what I made."

Maya's body never felt so weak. She wanted to grunt as if throwing a shot put and land a punch on the doctor's face but could not.

"I'm here to say goodbye. We are leaving town. You'll want to chase us, but you won't be able to."

"Where is she? What did you do with her?" Maya managed a question.

"Prepare yourself for the truth. Your daughter is okay. Follow me."

The doctor turned, no fear that Maya would attack from behind, and they walked to her car. The doctor popped open the trunk, and inside, some sort of contraption, a tiny case, tubes leading inside. Reminded her of a coffin of some sort, but with airflow to keep you alive.

To keep her daughter alive.

The doctor opened the lid, and her child was there before her, already grown a few inches in the last few days. Her chest moved in slow, rhythmic breaths, her eyes closed, in seemingly peaceful dreams. She was some science experiment, a lab rat waiting for the trials to begin.

"I owe you the truth. She's being fed, treated better than any child on this earth ever born. Her name is Lilith. Remember her fondly.

"You will miss her, and may try to follow us, but you'll be unable to. Her scents will be undetectable. She will be bathed in tomato paste, placed in air-tight containers. If you think you're on our scent, I'll do you a favor and let you know that you are mistaken, so save your time and efforts. Any lead you have is a false one.

"You should be proud, though. All the other children born in that room have been discarded as junk. But yours… yours is magnificent. You truly are the best mother out there. If you miss her too badly, and feel you can't go on, I wanted to give you something."

The Doctor presented a syringe.

"Luminex. We perfected this as we perfected this child. Shot into your muscle, it will dullen your gifts, but straight into your heart, and it will fill your aorta and stop your heart completely. The only way to stop it from beating for good."

Maya took the syringe in defeat, and as the doctor drove away, Maya doubled over in pain, hating the feel of the sun on her back. If she could only summon the might of days before she would fight, but instead, she curled onto the pavement right there and waited to melt into the asphalt.

But she wouldn't melt, she would be tended to by some good Samaritans who saw her on the ground in the parking lot as the funeral let out. They placed a hand on her shoulder, asked if she was alright. They told her it was a hotter than normal day, maybe get some water, and waited until she promised to hydrate and walked away.

She had no place to go but home, inside her house, just a piece of furniture gathering dust.

But when the moon started to shine and her senses awoke, she returned to the church and found herself more human prey to feed her hunger. She devoured the worst ones, the insidious evil ones living in a disguise. She moved about the city, howling in pain from the shadows, from the rooftops of abandoned homes, from backyards, in front of crack dens and dope houses. Each bit of pain she released was like a signal to her lost child, knowing that her voice would fade, but never be silenced.

The syringe Zita had given her gathered dust on her dad's old dresser, while Maya lived on and endured the constant longing.

14

2018 — KORI DRISCOE IN THE HOSPITAL TUNNELS

Kori had been sitting on the cold cement ground for so long the moisture had penetrated her jeans and was soaking her skin. The darkness surrounding her was pitch black, and she sensed more light with her eyes closed than with them open. This room, this whole hallway, was hidden. Nobody would find her here. She had only found it by mistake.

Now, like juices from a piece of meat, the hospital was leaking.

Every time she moved, just a tiny bit, she heard the clank of chains from one of the creatures in the blackness, lurching towards her. She dared not stretch out a leg or an arm, for some were so close she could feel their breath. Hot, rancid, acidic.

The image she caught of them in that instant of lantern light before it crashed to the ground showed they were humans, or part human. Either being stuck here for years had turned them savage, or they'd been born that way.

Did Dad chain them up, or someone else?

She picked up tiny bits of rubble from the ground and gently tossed the little stones around her, first one direction then another, trying to map out her territory, trying not to anger them too greatly. Some rocks fell to cement, but most hit flesh and were met with a snarl from the creature they landed upon.

Easily, a dozen of them surrounded her. Imprisoned, and dependent on her dad for their fate. In some ways, she was just like them. Kori pleaded with her dad, standing guard at the doorway.

"Dad, what the fuck happened to you?" she asked, hoping he would hear that she was no longer ten years old.

"I know you're suffering, Dad. You hate this. You're alone. This is torture, I can *feel* it. We can't give up, we can find help for you. Hades wants to see you. Even Mom wants to see you. It's been so long. Do you remember walking at Maybury in the winter, and you insisted on both of us testing the ice? *We didn't fall through.* You remember making brownies all night and then running out to Meijer's for ice cream at 3am because *a la mode or nothing*? Do you remember Hades as a puppy..."

She kept pelting him with memories, talking to the darkness, trying to stir something inside, but his only answer was; "That wasn't me. This is me, and these are my kind."

My kind.

She would rather kill herself than be caught in the grasp of one of *his kind*. But in some ways, she'd been in this fight before, with creatures unseen, a room unsafe, a dad unwilling. In that way, this hospital dungeon was the same as the house she'd been born into, only the front door escape route had been blocked.

Now she might die here, and she remembered a time when this was exactly what she had wanted—to leave her dead body forever inside Northville Psychiatric, never to be found.

Five years ago, she had purchased a Gatorade, a Snickers bar and an Exacto knife at Walgreens. Then she hitched an Uber ride to nearby the hospital grounds and walked the final mile; that way her car would be parked at home once the missing person search began, and they would never search the abandoned hospital.

She'd ventured to the most isolative part of the tunnels she could find and cuddled into the shape of a fetus. Thick bits of dust floated in the air, memories of the patients stuck inside, perpetually lost and suffering. This thick essence would be her new blanket. Her blood would spill and stick to her Dad's soul like a barnacle into eternity.

She had held the knife over blue vein under trembling wrist. Waiting, thinking, letting the history of emotions from these hallways seep inside her. She needed to slice *down* her vein, not across. All her research said that was the way to really bleed out. She softly traced the vein with the tip of the Exacto knife, not puncturing yet, just relishing the tiny scratch, trying to summon an angel or demon to give her a tiny push to make the incision.

But the voices seemed to whisper in her ear — or better yet, listen to her.

There are more miles left to your journey. Answers down the road. You're not done yet.

Instead of slicing her vein, she moved the knife up from her fragile wrist to the sturdy meat of her thumb and made a small cut. A cathartic release came out in droplets of blood, drip-drip-drip, onto the ground, a baptism, before moving on.

It was like a test she passed.

And now she learned that her dad had been nearby the whole time.

I could smell it when you left your blood here, he had said.

He never tried to stop her, did he? He just let her suffer. Never once offered the salvation of being discovered, telling her, *I'm here Kori, all fucked up and so you don't want any part of this, but I'm here, so please move on.* Nope, he let her suffer, and let her try to die.

Let her become more like him.

Maybe she had to really feel what he was before she could save him. He'd encouraged her to work in a vet clinic, as if that was the only way she'd understand the kind of animal he was. The only way she'd save him.

Three times she had found Dad after a suicide attempt, the last time when she had walked through the front door on Thursday after school, 3:17pm, and Dad's body was lying on the floor in the front room. A series of orange vomit puddles soaked the carpet, the largest one near his mouth. The putrid scent made Kori nauseous as she bent down and placed a finger on his jugular.

She felt a pulse, his skin was warm, his chest rising from lungs that were still breathing despite his best wishes. She called 911 and spoke the script once again, the inevitable repeated scene of ambulance with neighbors watching her dad get carried out on a stretcher. Mom stood by in bewilderment, arms akimbo, like a supervisor watching staff do the work they could not do on their own.

It was Kori's job to clean up the flaming orange vomit

stain from the carpet that her mom wouldn't touch. She scrubbed it with dish soap and elbow grease but couldn't get it clean. Every day the stain was a reminder, and sometimes she'd stare at the discolored splotch and imagine the tiny bits were alive, parts of Dad's guts growing into a human clone made of magnificent rainbow-colored sickness.

When Dad came home from the hospital a week later, he looked at the carpet stain in confusion, a tilt to his head for a better angle, wondering how the stain got there. His sickness came with amnesia, vague memories of previous lifetimes, a distance from what he'd done. He forgot old selves, constantly changing with a brain forging ahead, and every depressive dip that lead to thoughts of suicide would be followed with an elevation, a rise into new heights of mania.

Mom fell in love with his mania before it turned deadly. The stories she told of their lives together, her own eyes lit up talking about driving Route 66, about hiking with their tents on the back. Dad playing his acoustic.

Back then, Mom radiated warmth rather than the cold slab that now seemed forever fractured and alone. Kori loved her, wanted her to find the love and peace she deserved, but did not want to go to Florida with her. *You remind me of your father, I see him in you*, she said more than once. Not going with her to Florida was doing her mom a favor.

When Dad was on fire, Kori enjoyed the fabulous adventures and times of laughter. Sometimes they'd bake for hours and have flour fights until their shirts were full of handprints, white dust in their hair, both of them looking like grandmas. The fights never ended with a winner, just both of them doubled over in laughter.

Do we really need this many cookies? Of course, they did, so they mixed more batter, new ingredients, while Dad told his favorite mythology tales, set the timer and put in four trays at a time, went on trips to the store, (we'll be back in time), and then they ate cookies warm and moist right out of the oven. Kori went to bed with Dad still baking, woke up to a cookie being presented for breakfast, Dad saying, "Come on, taste this one, I used apple sauce instead of sugar." Then he asked her to sing along to acoustic songs like "Wreck of the Edmund Fitzgerald." *Fellas, it's too rough to feed ya*—but never once finishing the song because he got impatient and moved on to play another. *We need to get out. You need to get out,* and in his eyes he had the beam of love that shined, a kaleidoscope that she hasn't seen since.

Now his eyes were cold and piercing, a whole new color from whatever they did to him in this hospital dungeon.

"You should have left me to die," Dad said from the doorway out of the blackness, as if he could hear Kori's memories. "You didn't need to call for help so fast. You made a mistake. Ain't no use, living this life in conditions like mine. That's why I tried to kill the other baby girl of mine. Tried to do her a favor. Her mom don't think so."

"Do you remember playing guitar for me?"

"Aye, sure do. Strumming strings, I hit notes of pain to make joy and notes of joy to make pain. It's all the same, see? Just a yin yang circling until the center sucks you in. I'm down here, sucked in. That wasn't me—this is me, and these are my kind. Maybe ain't fair to have you sit there alive and scared and for them to listen to those thumps we hear from inside your chest. They want to take a taste of a heart while it's still beating and I ain't given them that in all these years."

Dad started humming to himself, restless, and his feet shuffled, pacing in small steps one way, then quickly back another.

She followed his movement with her ears. The same pattern repeated, again and again, while she grew hungry, thirsty, empty, until finally, a change in the pattern. Something different. He walked a bit out of the room. She heard his footsteps move down the skinny hallway.

Maybe he needs to *get out.*

She prepared to dash to her escape, mapping in her mind the way through the darkness out the door, but before she could move, she heard him returning.

He was dragging something along the pavement.

She heard him grunt and then the unmistakable sound of

a mass being hurled.

Thump.

It landed on the ground. *The body of the security guard,* was all Kori could think, and then the metal chains were yanked and started clanking, the beasts stretching them with all their might. Cries of anguish from those who couldn't reach the piece of meat, and the chomping noise of those who could.

The sounds of the feast filled the room, and she couldn't stop her mind's eye from seeing what she heard, from imagining which part was being eaten, which piece of flesh or bone, by the sound of the teeth ripping and chewing, and knowing that their next bite might be from her.

If one gets close, I'll fight back, I'll poke out their eyes, or go for their necks. I know how to fight.

But not against these kinds.

If I am going to die, I hope I die fast.

Don't just sit here, do something. Attack life, it's going to kill you anyways.

With the noise of them eating as cover, Kori bent her knees, got her feet solid under her, and rose to stand straight.

She plotted the course of her escape through the darkness. First, she would dash to the door, and then when his arms reached for her, she'd duck underneath, then sprint past him down the hallways, back into the familiar tunnels. Then up the metal rings to the surface, off through the woods to a warm hug for Hades. She'd send help to these hospital tunnels. Authorities in uniforms would medicate her dad and euthanize these beings.

Dad would go to jail for murder. He killed the security guard. He'd be happier in jail than here.

The pavement under her had the wetness of clay, and it helped her feet grip. She quietly stood up, waited to see if he noticed. One soft step forward, so small, nearly noiseless, moving slightly towards the last place she heard his voice by the door. She waited a long time in between steps, long enough to make it seem she wasn't moving at all, hoping her heart would stop, would slow, because *it was making too much noise.*

She would dash by him in the doorway. She couldn't hear

his voice anymore, but could feel his breath. His scent like rusted metal, his bones still crackling like the sound a dying bonfire makes when there's only red-hot embers.

There's always a door to escape. She knew how to survive. She'd live through Dad's manic energy and always found a refuge.

If I can't save him, I can survive him.

Steps through the dark, the air alive, she became a part of it, swimming softly, ready to sprint free, the exit so close.

"Damn you've gotten tall, Kori."

Dad could see everything.

The words crushed her hopes that he'd be taken by surprise, but she dashed through the dark anyways, and in just a few short steps, her bad shoulder crushed against the wall near the doorjamb, and her body pinballed right into him. Big arms, no balance, no time to duck.

He pulled her into him, another embrace. His body was so warm, his huge arms pulsating with energy and rage and muscles, skin as rough as the concrete walls. She wanted to beat against his chest but he clutched her limbs so tightly she couldn't move.

She was helpless to save him, helpless to save herself.

He had me. He's always had me. I've always been inside these arms.

"You have grown strong, my girl, you really are growing into one of my kind," he said, and with one final grunt, he gripped her with his claws and tossed her back inside the room.

For just a moment, she was suspended in air, completely cut off, nothing solid to hold her, falling as if into an eternal well, and then a cold landing on the dungeon floor, the clamor of a dozen chains clanking, beasts reaching towards her sprawling body. She wished in that instant she was *one of his kind*, because then they would have lived together as a family. Stayed together. Taking care of each other, never to be in this moment, so much misunderstanding.

And if she were *one of his kind*, she might be able to fight off the creatures attacking her from all sides.

One scratched at her leg and ripped a slit in her jeans. Another sliced down her face with a snarl. *Riipppp*. The claw tore into her flesh so fast she was sure it missed — until warm fluid dripped down her cheek. One big bloody teardrop.

She found her footing in a desperate instant, knew she had to move or would be their prey. She broke free and ran right back her dad's way.

Right back into his chest this time, not even trying to dodge him, but running into his grasp, the way she always had for years. This time when he grabbed her, she wrapped an arm around his neck and squeezed. She would refuse to let go, refuse to be pushed away.

I'm holding you, Dad. I'm not letting go.

"Kid, it's okay. You need to let me go."

No, she didn't. She squeezed as hard as she could, but her grip on him wouldn't hold. She felt his body slithering, changing, mutating, and she wanted to hug the dad she knew right out of him.

But it wasn't there. It was slipping as he pushed, about to toss her back to fend for herself. This time, all of the monsters were watching. Waiting. She could hear them panting, chains clanking, just rabid dogs waiting for their meat. Second course.

15

"Of all your scars, this one is my favorite," Lilith said as she studied the raised lump of pink flesh on Mama Zita's arm. The scar extended from the thick of her thumb up to the middle of her forearm.

Lilith lay sideways in the passenger seat, her legs folded and her feet dangling near the door. Her head was resting on the center console, her seatbelt fastened across her waist but rendered useless.

Mama Zita had been driving for six hours straight, and every new position Lilith took to get comfortable was held shorter than the last. She looked for anything to distract her attention. License plate games, counting cattle, listening to an audiobook Zita said would teach her about balance. All of it lost her interest.

All except Mama Zita's scar which seemed alive and throbbing. Lilith loved the way it was raised out of her skin, thick and meaty. It seemed the scar itself was steering them across the country. Lilith reached out a finger and traced the wound with her fingertip.

"Why do scars feels so smooth?"

Zita stared ahead, as if the truth to every mystery lay down the road, a place they might never meet, before giving an answer. "Scars are tougher than skin. You get hurt enough, you become made of scars, then they can't hurt you any longer."

"I bet this one hurt the most," Lilith said. She'd seen the other scars, the slices down Zita's thighs, her chest, the one across her back, but none were more alive than the one on her forearm.

"It only hurt because the person who did this to me was supposed to care for you. To love you. But look what your mom did to me instead. She hurt me. She hurt us."

The scar felt like a smooth snake trapped and slithering inside her skin, and Lilith wondered what her mom and dad did to cause this. Some sort of blade, it must have been, a sword, or maybe a knife. Zita only told her it cut through her arm so deeply she can no longer make a fist. Mama Z would never tell her the rest of the story.

Lilith imagined her parents in her mind's eye with weapons in their hands. She could never see their faces. Even in the numerous drawings she did when she was younger, the faces were never clear, but she always felt their coldness and the wounds they caused.

"Nobody knows where they are now," Zita had told her more than once, "or what they will do if they find you. That's why you need me. I was there when you were born, I worked in the hospital, and it was a treasure to keep you. I took you to California to keep you safe."

Lilith heard the roaring blast of an engine from behind them, like a monster giving chase across the country and closing in. She sat up in her seat and looked out the back window.

Two motorcycle riders, a man and a woman, drove up right behind them. They changed lanes, riding in unison, accelerated, and then kept pace in the lane to their left.

They wore no helmets, and the wind blew against their faces tightening their skin against their skulls. The man turned to look into their car, and Lilith felt his gaze like an X-ray shooting through her, skinning her alive. Nothing left to make a scar out of, just her guts.

The man had a grey beard splotched on his face. Black tattoos covered the length of his arm. Dark sunglasses kept his eyes hidden and he wore his leather vest like armor ready to do battle.

She was about to learn the answer to the question she'd been asking Mama Z all her life: *"What will Mom and Dad do if they find me?"* Because this was Mom and Dad right next to them, ready to run their car off the road and kill her like Mama Z said.

She was sure of it.

As if in response to tell her she was wrong, yet again, the

motorcycle engines roared, gas exploding in the incinerator, and they shot forwards. She watched them fade up the road in front of them. They were just two regular people. Another daydream nightmare that meant nothing, and she waited for her pulse to slow.

Zita kept her gaze straight forward, always with a squint.

"Do you ever feel your parents? Feel them coming for you?" Mama Zita had asked her more than once. *"If so, let me know right away."*

I feel them now. I always start to feel them, she wanted to say, *but the injection of Luminex makes me forget.*

"Are we there yet?"

"Not yet. We need to make the Mississippi. We have reservations at a little place. We need to be near the middle of the country, things will be in balance then. The outside, the fringes are coming soon enough."

Balance. Like having two parents, one on each side, instead of a doctor. Instead of a Mama Z. Instead of being sick.

The badlands of Dakota had given way to green landscape. Lilith started counting white stripes on the road as they passed, doing her best not to miss one, but her brain always went blank if she tried to think too fast. After twenty or thirty she had to shut her eyes since the numbers stopped making sense.

She turned the radio to AM and listened to the news, switching the dials, and the noise was just as fuzzy as her head. Mama Z kept driving, and it felt they were about to go off the edge of the world until, finally, Lilith could feel the car slowing, and they turned into their destination for the night.

The motel was a one-story, U-shaped building. The green doors looked like a hundred eyes watching over the parking lot. One part of the lot was full of truckers, the other full of motorcycles. Some riders were standing by their bikes, talking with wild hand gestures, biking outfits with patches sewed on jackets, promising allegiances. Other bikers ducked inside their rooms doing private things.

Lilith got out soon as the car stopped and soaked in the

fresh air. The air greeted her like it missed her just as much. Her legs creaked as she straightened them, and she followed Zita into the motel lobby.

A coffee machine with an empty glass pot, stained black on the bottom, sat on the counter. The walls were brown rustic paneling, and a stand full of pamphlets and promises of attractions nearby. The woman behind the desk looked up at them and Lilith saw her face turn to shock, wondering if she needed to grab her gun.

Lilith knew why.

She'd seen this look many times before. The woman's eyes darted to Zita, back to Lilith, then Zita, ping-pong style, trying to figure out why this white woman was with this brown-skinned girl.

"You and your...*daughter*?" the clerk asked, as if giving them a room depended on the right answer.

"Yes, one room, and yes, she's mine."

That was always her answer. *She's mine.* Zita's skin was a faded yellow, hers a richer brown. It announced to the world that this was not her daughter when people gazed at them in grocery stores, dentist's offices, and watching parades. They didn't seem fully of this world, always visitors to places, and Lilith was always the sick one. *My skin is stained because I am sick inside, different from you all.*

"I wanted a place that was empty," said Mama Zita counting cash from her wallet, "but this parking lot looks the opposite of empty. The place is full."

"Harley Fest in Sturgis. These bikers are heading back home. Just a bunch of New York or Chicago folks working in offices, just putting on airs trying to be bad-ass. They love their neckties more than their leather. You been to Sturgis?"

We're going to Michigan, Lilith wanted to say with excitement but stopped herself. *Blend in. Don't draw attention,* she'd been told. *We've already stopped too many places.*

She loved some of their stops. All the knickknacks at Wall Drug, such a fantastic store, like nothing she'd ever seen. The Badlands is a terrain so rough nobody could live there, a place just as lonely as she was. The white presidential faces on Mount Rushmore made her think of her parents watching her from the sky above; and nearby, the mountain sculpture of Crazy Horse. She'd wanted to get a closer look because Crazy Horse seemed just like her. Someday, when the artist was done sculpting, Crazy Horse would wake up and rip himself right out of the earth and show everyone what *crazy* really meant.

Crazy Horse was perhaps sick, too.

"Don't worry about them bikers. Police come by here so much and ask me to stop the human trafficking and the drug addicts. That's their job. All I do is stand here, take the money, give you a key, let you do what you do behind closed doors, then clean your mess when you're gone. You two will be fine."

Zita was finally handed two electronic key cards and they wheeled their luggage and supplies to their room and opened the green door. The noise of the bikers went silent when the door shut. As always when they traveled, Lilith never unpacked, just zipped open her suitcase, pulled out some boyshorts that she wore for pajamas, and lay on the bed as if it were the prize for being trapped in a car.

"Lil', don't lay on the cover, at least sit on the sheets. Stay on that cover and you'll be covered in the worst kind of germs."

Lilith expected her to say that, but stayed on the cover for a few moments longer out of spite. She'd roll the bedspread up and toss it on the floor, eventually. It was routine, same as Zita preparing the syringes full of silver Luminex in the chamber, holding it in the air and popping out the bubbles, and then asking Lilith to show her the thick of her thigh.

Each time before injecting, Z would remind her: *Your parents gave you this sickness, and I am here to take it away.* And by the time she was done talking, in an instant, the medicine would be in her body. Lilith could feel it circulate, or imagined she could, first through the big passageways, then the tiny capillaries, then turning her thoughts to lead. Bogging them down. A wet cement dream.

Your parents are going to be punished for what they did. The universe will make them bear their burdens tenfold.

Zita had the syringe ready to fire, but before she could take the next step, her cell phone rang. Mama Z actually answered the call. She rarely answered. Lilith caught part of what he was saying.

"Should be there in sixteen hours. Yes… drive straight when we leave in the morning…I can't take it on a plane…yes, it's full tomorrow night…. demolition starts when I say it can. Read your messages. Dammit. Hold on!"

Mama Z put the phone against her leg, picked up a hotel key card off the counter, and said without looking, "I need to step outside for a second. Just one fast phone call. But get off the covers, okay? You've already got all those germs on you."

Mama Z opened the door, letting the cool air come into the room when she walked out. The heavy door closed with a boom, Zita got sucked out into the night, and Lilith was alone inside behind closed doors.

16

ZITA OUTSIDE THE MOTEL DOOR

Outside the motel room, and dusk had quickly given way to the dark of night. A slight breeze swept over Zita from the nearby river, but the cooler air couldn't cool her anger. She was sure the phone call wasn't even needed. She cussed at Carter in her head.

Demolition was to begin as planned. They were to start with Building A, but only when she gave the final notice, and once she did, it would start within twenty-four hours.

And then all of them, *all of them,* would be destroyed. Buried in the rubble.

Sure, she was later in getting back to Michigan than intended, but she wanted to soak in every last minute with Lilith. The fantastic specimen had no idea what was coming.

She walked across the parking lot, away from a lit-up party store near the road, because she needed privacy. But before she dialed, she had to figure out what to say. Threaten or inspire him? The man needed to be dealt with, but with carrot or stick?

Lilith would be scared to leave the motel room alone, Zita knew that. She'd pounded that message home to her, again and again, but she was sure Lilith's mind would start wandering, tiny roots that branched out and needed to be killed, or better yet, frozen, until the time came. For now, she would keep medicating. The elixir was precious, and airport agents at security would certainly question the liquid, so they had to drive everywhere.

She pulled out the two syringes from her pocket, (always keep one extra, just in case). She gave one a quick tap-tap with her finger, put them back in her pocket, and moved on. The needle tips were safely capped, because all it took was a tiny prick to take hold. Zita had given Lilith countless dosages of Luminex through intramuscular injections, but now only a few more until the deadly shot into her heart.

Just a few days left to live, Lilith, but you've had a full life already.

Sometimes death is the best kind of treatment available. It is much more noble and ethical than trying to treat someone's illness the same way over and over again and making things worse, like had happened with Zita's own mother.

The final plunge of the Luminex into Lilith's heart would feel tragic, and Zita promised herself she would be there for the young girl in her final moments. She would look right into her baby's eyes so she wouldn't be alone as she slipped off to a permanent sleep. Zita had been around enough cold doctors who lacked empathy, and would not become like them.

These were the tough decisions she'd been making for years.

The euthanasia would certainly be harder than the simple procedure to take Lilith's eggs after a few rounds of fertility drugs. The anesthesia for the extraction was simple, just a small bit of Propofol had not only kept the young girl under, but also made her memories blur. Then, in-vitro fertilization, embryo transfer into Doctor Zita's own uterus, and...

Success! Pregnancy. It had taken. *I've grown a specimen. A perfect specimen. Fixed of all defects.*

Doctor Zita was pregnant with child. A new kind of child, the next generation, and now she needed to eliminate those who were lesser—including Lilith, her best work by far. Lilith was so refined compared to the abominations still left in the hospital basement.

Now she was traveling back to the hospital to take care of them, put them out of their misery, and end Lilith's life.

"S'cuse me... S'cuse me... You holding?" A voice interrupted her walk. "I know you're holding. I saw you with them needles, I saw you pack them pockets. You got a habit, dontchu? Come on baby, share just a bit."

Zita hadn't even seen the man sitting on the pavement until she was nearly upon him. His body took shape out of the shadows. His hair was stringy, his skin greasy. Tentacle fingers wrapped upon his knees, and his eyes looked her over, examining for weakness. He was expecting fear, she knew this, but seemed surprised when she stood her ground. If this man only knew the people she'd shared a room with, desperate souls full of such mental anguish, neural pathways as deep and black as the universe, the kind only experienced by those who've roamed the locked hallways of hospitals and moved through its bowels.

"I've got nothing," she said, not looking into his eyes, feeling them on her as she moved on.

"How about that girl. I saw you with her. I can get some fat stacks of cash and—"

"Trust me, you don't want to pay that price."

Zita wanted to give him a roundhouse kick to the teeth, but instead moved on with a quicker pace. She needed to get back to the room. The glow of the moon above had turned surrounding clouds aqua blue, but it was outshined by her cell phone in hand and ready to dial. She could hear the rushing waters of the Mississippi nearby, and felt she was on her own steamboat, lighting out for new territories, new frontiers, as soon as she took care of business back home.

What would it be like to go back to Northville Psychiatric? It had been a dozen years. All she'd seen since then is bloggers' accounts of trespassing on the abandoned facility's property. They gave tips on how to avoid security guards, and showed pictures of the morgue, the theater, the seclusion rooms, but most of all, the tunnels underneath that connected each building.

It's not safe, she thought to herself as she read each blog post, and when the blog postings stopped abruptly, she pondered the reason why.

Part of her was sad the huge facility was being demolished, but she'd safely secured the best parts. Demolishing the hospital would wipe away the hurt, and a phoenix would rise.

Zita would do the same to her own childhood home, if she could, for in some ways, she grew up in a smaller version of the hospital. A house full of hurt, painted in the color of her mom's mental illness, and an unfinished basement with concrete walls underneath.

Each morning, and each night, for so many years growing up, Zita used to put the pills in her mother's mouth. She could still picture the Depakote sticking to the pink taste buds. Each time, it felt as if Mom was being slowly poisoned. Mom swallowed each pill with water and with hope, and afterwards her mouth seemed stuck in a silent scream.

If she could only get her mom to release that scream, then all the bipolar sickness would come out, but instead, it was as if her mouth had been zippered shut and the illness locked inside.

"Mom, it will get better," Zita promised, but she didn't really believe.

Her last image of Mom was on the front porch. Cars passing by, Mom eyeing them suspiciously. She was smoking a cigarette, exhaling the smoke as far into the heavens as her lungs would allow, blowing it up with all her might. An empty brown prescription bottle sat next to her, keeping her company, and the white cap of the bottle alongside.

"I took all the pills for you, every last one," her mom said, and then after a wry smile, began vomiting on the porch.

They were off to the hospital where they would charcoal Mom's stomach, yet again. Instead of packing Mom's things to send to the hospital, as usual, Dad packed for himself.

"I can't do this. I'm leaving. You fix her." And he left Zita alone.

You fix her.

Zita marched forward to the beat of those words the rest of her life.

You fix her.

Her dad never returned. She waited a few days, going to school, pretending it was temporary, but she could feel it was different this time.

She told Mrs. Holden, her English teacher, the only one she trusted, the one who taught her about Thoreau and Emerson, and Mrs. Holden walked her down to the social worker. Mrs.

Holden waited with her and then followed up for months in ways that most teachers would not. There are helpers everywhere if we look. People who do things extraordinary and go beyond expectations and conventions.

Zita wanted to be a Mrs. Holden.

Her mom lost custody, and Zita grew up in foster care, certain that if she could fix her mom then she could go home. Then Dad would come back.

She lived in three different foster care homes and went to two different high schools. By eighteen, the state supported her with supervised independent living and a case manager. One day, that case manager tapped on her shoulder to let her know mom was dead.

You fix her.

She was going to find a way to fix bipolar disorder. To siphon out the worst parts, and make the best parts boil to the top. She had to try something new, because *foolish consistency is the hobgoblin of little minds*. The same efforts bring same results. Her mom had died, unfixable.

Doctor Zita had seen patients mindlessly prescribed the same medications despite their complaints of debilitating side effects. These complaints were ignored, disregarded, as if they weren't humans, as if they weren't mothers and daughters, loved ones and magnificent souls. She saw the best minds destroyed by bad treatment.

Zita was turning psychiatry upside down, and she realized how misunderstood she would be, like Jesus and Galileo, both killed for their wisdom. *To be great is to be misunderstood,* was something Emerson said, and something she accepted. *Every pure and wise spirit that ever took the form of flesh* was treated in such manner.

Whoever walked this path, walked alone.

She moved through the motel parking lot under the darkening sky, finally on her way back home, back east to the rising sun, after years of hiding. She would give birth to a child, a new kind of life, but before that, some older lives needed to be put down.

Carter, the CEO of the demolition company, just needed to accept his payment and follow her plan.

We need to cut off the initial specimens in the basement. They can't escape. We left them there, and they will not die. Their transformed DNA would persist, and they would rage and want to the cycle of the moon.

Maya needed to die, too, and Lilith would be perfect bait. It was a great sadness that Maya never got to see Lilith grow, but Maya was really just a midwife in a sense. Zita had raised the child splendidly, as promised, just waiting for her to fully flower so she could extract her egg. And now she would put Lilith to sleep, and honor her memory and sacrifice.

Painlessly.

Doctor Zita stopped her walk at the parking lot edge under the moonlit sky, ready to call Carter Demolition, and that's when she was assaulted.

An arm reached around Zita's neck and squeezed, cutting off her wind.

Maya, an attack from Maya, was Zita's first thought. She'd been living in fear of such an attack since the day she left with Lilith to the west coast.

No, not Maya. I'd be dead by now.

But there was strength, and swiftness in the bony arm. His elbow locked around her neck, squeezing against her wind pipes. She grabbed at, but it was tight as a noose. Too tight to budge.

I underestimated the skinny heroin man.

Zita kicked. She bucked like a rodeo bull. She tried to shake off this man, who had her in his grasp. His body odor was putrid, the familiar sweaty poison of desperation and rage. She'd been in a hundred hospital scrums with people just like him.

Lilith, alone in the room, with no Luminex in her veins.

She had to break free. God, she'd been so careful up to this point. She'd only missed one dose. Lilith was four years old then, and had scaled up the walls, speaking with language that she later forgot once she'd been dosed up again.

Gasping for air, Zita reached a hand into her pocket, grasped one of the needles, popped the cap with her thumb, and held it in her fist. One thwack of the syringe into the man's leg would do it. She held the syringe like a knife, ready to assault.

Just as she went to plunge it into his body, he grabbed her wrist. His fingers clamped on her ligaments and he made it swing away from him and towards her own body. Rather than stab into the leg of her attacker…

Thwack.

Cold metal pierced into her own flesh. The syringe had stuck into the top of her thigh. It went through her jeans, through her skin, into the muscle, and while not injected with the full dose of the Luminex, it was enough.

Her body went limp. The attacker released his grip in confusion as she went to the ground. He looked both ways, no witnesses, and then he scurried off.

Zita was left on her knees in the pavement.

My God, what has happened?

The moon was the only witness to the attack. It shined above her, one day from glowing full, but the cycle for hunters was here. The time for gifted humans to rise up and move about the earth in all their splendor and glory, and Zita instead was about to be knocked out.

This wouldn't kill her. They did trials before with a sample group, those not blessed with such extreme mania and mood swings. Regular folks. None died. All became lethargic, most became unconscious just moments after a dose. One needed to be intubated.

That will not be me, she thought, head spinning. She tried to fight it.

She would be okay. She would go back to her room. She would fight the Luminex and not pass out.

Spinning and spinning…the motel was flipping and flipping…

The cement ground didn't feel so bad, just a short rest, one minute wouldn't hurt. The weight of the silver medication closed her eyes.

Get ready, Lilith. The sickness your mom gave you. The one I tried to take away.

Get ready, it's coming.

17

LILITH IN THE MOTEL ROOM

Lilith pulled her legs up and wrapped her arms around them. She looked at her skin and the tiny hairs on her legs growing out her pores. Soon she'd have just as many pin-hole scars from the pokes of the needle. She was a pin cushion, but nobody could see her little hurts, nothing like the scars on Zita.

She better get off the bedspread before Mama Z came back. Her skin was barely touching the orange bedspread, how could it soak inside her anyways? She wanted to ask Zita this, and a thousand other questions, but the questions were washed away each night by the silver wave of liquid medicine put inside her.

Z wouldn't leave her alone in this room for long, so she peeled the covers back to the white sheets underneath and tossed the bedsheet on the ground.

She opened up the drawer of the bed stand and saw this room, like all the other motel rooms, had a Bible. She loved the pages of the Bible, always the thinnest of any, and she flipped through, never reading a word. The quiet of the room became more intense, like it'd been quiet so long that violins started playing from the walls to fill in the empty places, those little gaps in her thoughts that she didn't try real hard to figure out, because Zita did that.

She wouldn't do a thing until she got her medicine. Until then, life was on hold.

Part of her loved this moment of life more than any other, when the molecules in her head dissipated, bits of them separating from each other, breaking free. Sometimes she wished it would last longer, her thoughts spinning in chaos, atoms colliding, each one of her cells with their own little brains and thoughts, each one equally confused. She savored the time before the injection, because once the needle pierced her skin, everything slowed down and froze.

With each moment Zita was gone, (*longer than expected, where is she?*), the violins got louder, like an orchestra was inside the room next door, inside her own head, bouncing around her own skull. All of it so fast that she had to move each limb to keep up. Little tics in her body everywhere.

She couldn't take it anymore. She got up to pace from one wall to the next. She went to the window and opened the curtain. Far cross the parking lot, an occasional car zoomed by along the highway, headlights moving on to places elsewhere, and she wished she could go. The bright lights of a party store stood alongside the road. A man carrying a twelve-pack of bottled beer was walking back to his room. He could see her. She could see him.

She closed the curtain back up.

She was hungry, thirsty, craving sensation. She wanted some Chips Ahoy or Mountain Dew, or a cheeseburger with bacon. Just thinking of it made juices drip on her tongue.

Something was wrong.

An hour passed, but she knew her training. *Try to go unnoticed. Stay put.* How many times on their travels had she been told this?

But she had to move and pace when her thoughts went from one side of the room to the other. She wondered if she could inject herself but Mama Z had taken the syringe with her. Each moment she expected to hear the beep of the electronic key opening the door, then that suctioning noise it makes when it opens, followed by apologies for leaving her alone so long.

Instead, she listened to rattles from the rooms next to her, like the walls were thinning with each moment. She was inside the Bible, the walls just the thin pages. Words came to her. *Thoughts.* The history of all time when Jesus was crucified, when Jesus was born, before Christ was born, the Old Testament, in the beginning was the Word. Memories of those who slept there before, the pain of their lives became hers, just germs on the bedspread, waiting for a new host to infect.

Go to the front desk. Tell them she's missing. Go outside and find her. She's in trouble.

She got off the bed, opened the door and took a step outside. She still wore only the boxers and a green tank top, and the air had a cold nip to it, like opening up a freezer.

The heavy motel room door started swinging shut.

I need a key. I'm locking myself out.

She reached back to stop the door from closing and it slammed onto her fingers. Pain shot into her head with a jolt, but the pain...

The pain was so different.

So nice. *Exquisite*, a word she heard rich people say, but it was the one word that fit, and she wished she could do it again, and harder, and with each finger.

She placed the motel key in her waistband and went out into the night.

The parking lot was still, and the streetlights were no match for the moonlight which shined off motorcycle chrome making silver rainbows. The glow gave her energy and focus, and she could hear the Mississippi river flowing, massive and deep. Scents hung thick in the air as if she'd just walked into a flower shop.

Go to the lobby and report Zita missing.

No, don't let them know we're here.

The party store was the only destination that made sense. Lilith was pulled towards it. Plus, they'll have Dr. Pepper. She craved it. The sugar, the rush. Something to help her body catch up to her thoughts which were whirling faster, her mouth full of words she didn't know how to speak. Zita needed to figure it out for her.

The ding of a bell announced her arrival, and the eyes and ears of the cashier perked up with suspicion that only grew when they saw it was a brown-skinned girl, wearing a tank top and boxers.

She pulled a cold two liter of pop from the cooler. First one, then two, something to guide her on this new sea she was sailing on. She brought it to the counter, adding a Twix and three bags of Skittles from the candy shelf underneath. Dr. Pepper and

Skittles — the craving for them felt innate. She wished she could open them up now.

The cashier behind the counter assessed her loot as if he didn't approve. He paused. His paunch of a stomach looked like a four-month baby bump in his red Coca-Cola t-shirt.

"Who you with? Who's with you?" he asked, but kept talking before she could try to respond. "You need help, don't you? I think you do. You staying at the motel? Seen girls like you with a man by their side. Trafficking ain't cool. It ain't cool. This whole place ain't cool anymore. Dope addicts jumping and pimp's pimping. I can treat you better. I can treat you right and sweet as this candy. I promise."

She could smell the tobacco stuck on his skin and she thought of talking but couldn't speak the language of the words that wanted out. The electric zing of the party store lights hovered above her, and her skin felt like it was coming apart and something underneath was ready to burst. She had no way to stop it, and no money to pay for her candy, so she grabbed her stuff and headed for the door.

"You need cash, right? I live right by here, stay with me."

She didn't need to pay, she wasn't of his world, she was a hunter-gatherer and needed meat, needed sensation. The lizard brain would be fed.

"No need to pay, you can help me in other ways. I'll be right behind you. I'm watching you."

She did feel him watching her leave, but she needed to run, to move, things inside her were becoming so loose, rearranging, busting out the seams.

Could she even walk back?

What is happening to me?

The sickness, it's coming. It's oozing out of her and she had no medication, she knew this, but didn't want to turn back.

Rushing through the parking lot only made her want more.

She opened the door to the motel room, and on the floor, she saw them.

All of them squiggling. Microscopic bugs on the orange

bedspread waiting for her, swirling like yin-yang signs, circling and spreading and moving about each other. One big pool of germs looking for someone like her to latch on to, like a newborn to its mother.

But no Dr. Zita inside.

The night got darker, and she got stronger. She paced the room and didn't sleep, hungry for more than sugar, now she wanted meat. She imagined leaving the room and going back the way they came to the Badlands of North Dakota and living off the land.

No, don't leave.

Atoms in her brain and all the fluids lubricating her spine started to ooze like hot lava destroying anything in their way, demanding to be fed. She counted the tiles in the bathroom; how quick the numbers came to her, her brain calculating. The blood inside her became so warm she felt heat leaving her ears.

Muscles underneath her clothes started to bubble, to grow, pushing outwards. The elastic on her shorts expanding, the bra being pushed against skin, her flesh itself boiling, her fingers elongating into hardened cleavers, the mix of ecstasy and joy and rage. She wanted her parents with her then, her mom, her...

A knock on the motel door.

It sounded like a knock on her skull, but no, someone wanted into her Bible story.

"I know you're in there. I saw you. I know you're alone. I got what you need. I'm sweet. *Sweet as they come.* Let me in."

Let me in. Everything wanted *in*, and she needed out in the night, a hunger in her to eat, to feed. Her insides were so hollow with hunger.

She opened the door. The party store man with the red Coca-Cola t-shirt was standing there, and she read his whole history as fast as she read the words on his shirt. *Private parties in this motel complex. Young girl victims believing his forked tongue told tied-together truths.*

She could hear the man's heart thump, each valve open and close, the warm explosions of each beat, and the movement of the rich, red muscle pumping inside.

His brain had no time to react when her hand struck, and Lilith ripped open his jugular with her nails. She sprung forward and her mouth clamped down upon the spurting geyser of blood from his neck. So thick. So full of elixir. Blood like this was meant to nourish her spirit.

He really was sweet as they come.

He fell to the ground, and Lilith imagined unraveling his skin and eating the part of him she coveted most — the moist richness of his beating heart. His flesh was just the candy coating. Like a Skittle.

God did she feel alive, invigorated, and without the leaden dull of the medicine in her, the primal scream could not be held back. It exploded from her soul, and she howled in symphony with every beast in the land.

It caught the attention of Mama Zita, who was staggering back.

The energy beam of Mama Zita's eyes burned through Lilith, each sweat bead in Mama Z's pores pungent, as she ran across the parking lot to where Lilith stood over her kill. The body that lay in front of the motel door was ragged, bloody, lying in unnatural state, and Lilith stood over it, unashamed.

Mama Z stopped in front of Lilith, both of them looking at each other for the first time. Zita's scars glimmered in the moonlight. The dead tissue, once just a pink molten line that spread out across her arm, was now alive with the story of the moment the wound was first created. Like invisible ink come to life, Lilith could read its history, a thousand images shooting through her brain — cement walls of a hospital dungeon, humid air, blood and raw meat and silver mist.

Zita had been holding Lilith as an infant when the attack happened, when she got the wound that caused the scar. Her mother had swiped at Dr. Zita's arm to rip her child from Zita's embrace, slicing with precision to not hurt Lilith, but only sever muscle and make it impossible for Zita to hold her baby anymore.

Lilith felt stabbed in the gut by the sorrow of that day, the sorrow of her true mother. A mother whose beloved baby was being stolen. It was an attack born of love, a love that still exists.

So many lies. Years of lies.

Zita had been feeding her with medicine and lies. Lilith had no *sickness* – she had power, and that truth exploded inside her head and the rage was released from her lungs in another howl that pierced the night sky.

"Lilith. Listen to me. You're sick. I'm sorry I was away. Something happened. Show me your thigh."

Lilith tried to answer, but rather than words another howl rang out and floated to the heavens, like moon mist rising in the sky.

Zita flinched but remained steadfast. She reached her hand into her pocket and drew the syringe full of Luminex.

Lilith's talon fingernails, ready to slice Zita apart, stopped in the presence of the silver liquid. Her burning lava blood turned heavy in its presence. Each red platelet coursing through her veins felt threatened.

Zita lunged forward with the syringe, wielding it like a sword, stabbing it towards Lilith's chest. But the *sickness* remained safe, the *sickness* saved Lilith from death, because the syringe found only empty air. And before Zita could attack again, the twelve-year-old child had disappeared in a dash across the parking lot and found refuge in the riverside brush.

In the woods, Lilith heard the noises of ants marching and could smell the queen birthing her colony. She could sense each bit of foliage growing in millimeters from the previous night's rain. An opossum's nest was near the riverside; five females, four males, feeding in their mother's pouch. The river moved in a massive sweep, and Lilith felt every bit of life swimming below, catfish on the bottom sensed her presence, as she did theirs.

This river ran north and south but she needed to go due east, towards where the sun rises. Where her parents gave birth to her and still lived. Her own tribe. A mom who still loved her, missed her, the only one who could truly understand Lilith and didn't see her as *sick* and needing medicine.

Anger and rage burned up her spine, fueled by the glow

of the moon.

She would rip Zita apart someday, better yet, kill anyone that Zita loved. She would detect her scent no matter where she went. No longer were they like the mother and child who camped in the Grand Canyon, who drove along the west coast of California and listened to books on tape along the way. Lilith hungered to rip those scars back open, to finish the job her mom had started—but first, a bigger craving to fill. The gaping hole in her gut caused by the absence of her mom's love. Her real mom.

And her journey east began.

18

LILITH TRAVELS HOME

Lilith had traveled all night on the roofs of trucks. First, she had scanned the faces of the driver, knowing where they were heading in advance, then jumped upon the top of their rig and latched on for the ride. With each passing mile she was treated with a kaleidoscope of scents, each moment forward a hint of her birthplace up ahead, a salmon with the instinct to swim upstream to where it was hatched.

After she found herself close, she jumped from the rooftop and dashed street-side through the shadows, hiding from the light, aware of any threats. There were so many humans, and each of their beating hearts thudded like a drum, beckoning her with its beat. Part of her wanted to taste more human blood, but she had a bigger calling, so moved on.

Her home, the old hospital, was a beacon that pounded her senses, and she zeroed in until she found herself a mile away, drawn to a parking lot, and then face to face with a dog trapped inside a car. Same way Lilith had been trapped for the last dozen years.

Lilith and the canine beast gazed at each other through the glass. Lilith's eyes swirled with orange and yellow, soaking in all stimuli, the dogs eyes a reflecting black pool, looking for a savior. Both creatures had nostrils flaring, detecting scents, intentions, histories. The animal's scars where no fur grew told the story of her attack as a pup, when a larger dog, bred for slaughter, made to pull bricks on concrete sidewalks to strengthen its neck, injected with steroids, starved and savage, had attacked and nearly killed this animal in a dog-fighting den.

A bait dog that had survived. And now it was trapped.

The car window shattered on the first hit. The caged animal jumped out of the window and landed on the pavement. It bowed its head in a mix of fear and thanks, sniffed at this strange, exotic person, and when it felt safe to do so, dashed off into the forest.

Lilith was about to do the same.

Beasts are all being unbound tonight.

She followed the animal into the forest, and the woods accepted them both, each branch letting her pass freely, parting as if for Moses, as if it had been waiting for her. She came upon a fence, and with two fast strides and a leap she cleared it, landed on the other side, and galloped on towards the building.

She found a shadow that was the doorway, like a black hole into her past, and went inside. Each tiny bit of hair on her body stood on edge from the electricity in the air.

This was home, these dark caverns. This is what Mama Zita took her away from.

She moved about the hallways on floor three, then four, then six, going higher and higher. She dashed through the slanted beams of brilliant moonlight that shined through broken windows, fascinated by her new found power, no longer surprising her, it had found a home inside her birthplace.

She took refuge in a bedroom — the last man who had slept here had so many secrets, and she listened to them all. It was darker in the bedroom with the moonlight shaded, but she could still see just as sharp. She examined her arms — the muscle under the skin made it vibrate. Fingernails extending from her fingertips had hardened into daggers. Her teeth were just as sharp, and she felt each one of them with their own hunger, each sense so acute.

The Gods had graced her with gifts, and with those gifts, she felt the curse of patients from long ago all around her.

There was so much pain in these hallways. The echoes of screams still bounced off the walls, not just the kind that were propelled out one's throat, but those that imploded inwards, making internal organs wither. Their history was written in the concrete, like eternal spray paint, telling a thousand stories of patients come and gone. When it all seemed to peak, she wailed out into the night sky a howl that had been stuck in her throat, summoning all the kindred souls who ever walked these halls into her own spirit.

She had that power — to suck in the strength of every soul whose presence was nearby, to take that power with her.

Over time, she felt the power leaving her, by degrees, barely noticeable, but enough to warn her this wasn't permanent. *There — it left, just a bit. There — just a bit more.* This was temporary, this new palace of muscled armor, of perceptual powers, of cravings insatiable. It was only hours more in her grasp.

Gravity summoned her below and she bounded down stairs, descending underground to the tunnels. Her mom had been here years ago, and traces of her remained.

This was it. She was born nearby. Her senses rang like a cacophony of metal and concrete bashing. She remembered being held, feeding on the breast of her mother, but then her throat being squeezed, her wind being cut off. Someone was trying to kill her — *did* kill her, but who?

The Father — that's who.

She remembered the look in his eyes. Though she was days old, it stuck in her head. She'd not only been born here, she had died here. Her dad killed her, stopped her heart, and discarded her as dead. But soon her mind began working again and heart began beating.

The Father is still here.

She could smell him nearby. She swallowed the scent, and it went through her nostrils and dug its nails into her head, making her head bleed, with anger seeping from the cracks.

Her feet carried her with the swiftness of a gothic garden creature, down to the tunnels, where a person with a lantern walked right by her, unable to detect Lilith watching from the shadows. Lilith would follow her soon enough, but first wanted to soak in every memory of time she spent with her mother, when they lay together and fed from one another, before they were split and separated.

She wouldn't stop until they came back together.

19

Wrecking balls and cranes from Carter & Co Demolition loomed high outside, camped out night after night, largely alone besides the occasional security guard walking by.

The machines were ready to strike. The asbestos abatement was complete in some portions of the compound, but in others, all they could do was hope that the poison and illness trapped inside wouldn't infect the whole town of Northville. The whole state of Michigan. The atmosphere of the earth.

The walls were coming down.

Just underneath the surface, Kori Driscoe's arms were wrapped around her dad's shoulder but were slipping off his skin. His neck was moist with the humidity and sweat and slime of a dozen years from living in this tunnel, the last of the patients to leave. He was the caretaker of the beastly Vrykolakas, offspring from patients inside, genetic permutations gone wrong.

I'm holding you, Dad. I'm not letting go.

"Kid, it's okay. You need to let me go."

Let him go.

She had let him go. She'd let him leave their house manic a hundred times, following Mom's lead who had resigned to his condition and saw him as already dead. Mom wasn't part of his body, so she could move on, she *should* move on. But Kori couldn't go with her to Florida, couldn't let Dad go, so she tried to stay stuck to his body. It would take a god like Zeus to pull them apart.

Hungry beasts surrounded them in the darkness. The noxious metallic scent of their breath clouded the air. As her fingers slipped off her dad, she got ready to be devoured. The odor of their breath would be stained with her own organs soon, and their future exhales into this dungeon would be the spreading of her ashes.

Slipping, screaming, praying her dad would love her enough to hold on, she realized Dad was gone, his love was gone, only his sickness remained.

When your fears reach a certain terror, once it reaches its maximum, there's always someone that comes to help. As long as you do your part, they will do theirs.

And it did. The building responded again.

A screeching snarl, like a street cat wailing through the night. A creature attacked.

It sounded younger, fresher, but ferocious. Kori could sense its movements slashing through the darkness, moving with a fury too fast for her dad. When its nails sliced into her dad's hand, it first caught Kori's cheek, and cut her flesh with a burning sting.

First one side of her face sliced by the Vrykolakas, now the other side by this new creature. She was bloody but set free, safe in the doorway.

In front of her, she could almost make out the outline of her savior standing in the darkness. She seemed female, maybe a foot shorter and looking up at Kori. Her orange and yellow eyes sparkled, even in this darkness. There was something familiar in those eyes, and the two made short communion before the young thing went deeper into the room, and Kori was left with her dad's body on the ground.

Kori was free to escape but didn't. Instead, she took a knee next to her dad.

"God damn this life hurts," he said, voice gurgling with blood, fading. "Icarus crashed hard, sunk to hell."

His final words before she felt him fade to black.

Kori put her body on his chest in a hug. His bones were still sturdy and his muscles still strong but all of it starting to sink to the ground.

If she was stronger, she could lift him up and save him. If she was stronger, she could carry him away. Instead, she had to leave him there, certainly to die. She had caused this. If she'd only just stayed away.

She put a hand to her own cheek, matted her finger with

the blood that was oozing from the rip on her face, and she wiped it on Dad's cheek as if giving him war paint. A war that he had lost. *We've all let him down. All of us. Doctors and hospitals, wives and daughters.*

Inside the room, the creatures were now chirping, chains clanking as if celebrating the start of a new year. Noises of excitement and glee.

They were no longer on the attack, no longer chained to the walls, they were rejoicing.

Rising up among the cheers of the beasts came the unique sound of her savior howling wildly, her growls unmistakable among the more savage tones. This girl seemed more kind, and more Godly, than any of the Vrykolakas.

She remembered her dad's words. *I'm waiting on her, she's coming soon. We need a King Arthur to set them free.*

Kori took off running down the skinny, dark passageway, while behind her, the unbound Vrykolakas surrounded her dad's body. Fearful they'd give chase, she refused to turn around — but like her dad, they stayed in their room even when set free.

She scrambled through the thick gloom, fearful to pause and pull out her cell, so she grazed the wall with one finger for direction. She made it to the main tunnel and then ran towards the trace of light coming from the exit.

She arose from the tunnels as if rising from her grave, bursting forth to the fresh air.

Call 911, call 911. Her brain was on repeat as she rushed through the Evil Woods, branches reaching out and grabbing her, but none with thorns sharp enough to hook on. Brush at her feet, at her legs, but she ran, ran through it all, hoping the answer to her next move lay ahead, parked at Hawthorn.

What to tell them? The 'authorities?'

"There's a dead guard in the hospital. My dad's dying. There are people down there."

Maybe they can save him.

Then she remembered what he had said.

"You should have left me to die. You didn't need to call for help so fast. You made a mistake. Ain't no use, living this life in conditions like mine."

Out of the woods, huffing for air, her face bleeding more because rush of blood in her veins. Her car was still there waiting. Hades' fears of being left alone would be erased.

But when she got back, Hades was gone.

Shattered glass lay on the ground by her car from the broken passenger window. She stared at it in disbelief, the scratches on her face starting to sting from tears dripping. It was all falling apart, all getting demolished.

I have to find her.

Her eyes scanned in a circle, looking for Hades waiting nearby and to return, but nothing.

She shouted her name, "HADES!" certain she could hear, *unless someone took her and she's long gone.*

No, she has to be here. Her ears had certainly just perked up at the sound of her name and soon she'd come trotting out of the tree line. She waited and screamed, paced and hollered, but no sign of her beloved pet.

Near the entrance to the parking lot to Hawthorn, she saw cars turning in, other cars leaving. It was likely time for the employees' shift change. Would one of them help? Who helps in times like these, who would believe her and the strange things she's seen?

She reached in her car for a bottle of water and she emptied it, pouring some in her mouth, some over her face washing off the cuts. Both water and blood dripped down her chest.

Might need stiches, but not that deep. She was fine.

Her phone was at 30%, one text message from her mom saying "G'Morning. We R on the road. Vet techniciansorassistants. Not Veterinarians! I'll b lookin," and then a smiley face.

Kori walked back into the trees, where her spirit animal was surely roaming. Her steps became more cautious, her eyes scanning as she searched in a zig-zag, covering huge bits of territory, parts untraveled in the Evil Woods, but no sign of Hades.

It would be light soon. That will help, but with every

moment, it felt Hades became more lost. *With every moment, I'm more lost.* What were the creatures from the hospital going to do now that they were free? She was walking right back towards them. The only noise was the crunching of her feet over branches.

"Hades!" She yelled her name into the sky, and her voice seemed to summon dawn, for the sun was rising and day was breaking. Whoever said it was darkest before the dawn never knew real dark, the kind of dark that stays inside no matter what the sun brings.

She came upon the fence. If Hades had gotten this far, she would not have been able to go any further. She stared across at the hospital as if it held answers to where to look. The grounds were no longer lit by blue moonlight but by a rising yellow sun. The brick was soon exposed to the light, and once again, the hospital answered.

Someone was staggering out of the building towards her. It was moving unsteady on its feet, wavering, like a punch-drunk boxer. It collapsed to its knees, looked up to the sky, and then fell flat on the grass.

Kori waited to see if it would get back up. Nothing.

She bent the metal fibers back again on the fence and ran to where the body fell.

It was a girl, flat on her back, clothes ravaged. She wore a green tank top, shorts, and was maybe fourteen years old. She touched the girl's forearm. Her skin was warm, she could feel life inside, and her breathing was regular and rhythmic but her body wasn't stirring one bit. It seemed like a body stuck in a coma. Kori waited, touched her eyelid, just a bit, and pulled it back to reveal diamond black pupils in the middle swirling orange and yellow galaxies. Blood covered the girl's lips and neck.

This was no regular human. This was the girl who attacked her dad. Who saved her life.

Kori left her hand on the girl's shoulder, and then finally, her eyelids started to flutter.

Who are you and what are you and why are you here? All of these were questions Kori wanted to ask but all that came out was, "You're here?" Why are you here?"

"I was born here," she answered in a voice that didn't convince Kori she was human, for it came not from her mouth, but from somewhere deeper in her gut. Her face was twitching, and her presence itself felt sad. Kori could feel a loneliness.

"He loved me so he tried to kill me."

"Who?"

"Medusa Messiah."

Medusa Messiah. How could she know that phrase? She knows things, she's of this world. Born here.

Kori leaned over her, like a nurse at a hospital bed. She lay one hand on her forehead as if checking her temperature and to let her know she's not alone.

As the sun continued to rise, the girl's face continued to turn, losing its primitive shape, becoming more human in the light, the brows no longer as deep, her nose no longer with flared nostrils. Muscles faded to a slender girl, now looking younger than fourteen. Kori winced at the sound of her bones crackling inside her, shape-shifting into something new.

"Don't let her find me like this," she said with weak voice. "All those lies. She can't find me."

"Who?"

"Mama Zita. The doctor."

Her eyes closed again and her body became limp. Regressing. Defenseless.

Unlike her dad, the girl's body was small enough to carry, so Kori reached down and cradled her in her arms. She was remarkably light, and Kori moved on.

She propped the girl's head up with her elbow. The muscles that had been so powerful were now just that of a sturdy girl, her legs bouncing to the side with each step away from the hospital. When Kori came upon the fence, she used her back to bend it open, then kept walking through the woods. She took a couple of breaks by setting the girl softly back onto the ground, and each time she picked her back up she became a part of her again, like this was weight she'd carried before. The two becoming twins, shadow selves.

Taking her through the evil woods, she did her best to hurry, because Hades was gone.

She'd just traded out one creature for another.

It was full daylight when she got back to the car, and she partially expected a SWAT team waiting, ready to arrest her, ready to take care of everything; find her pet, save her dad, help the creatures inside, tell her mom everything was okay — do something. Instead, there was nothing. Nobody noticed the weight she was carrying.

How did Hades get out? She certainly didn't break the window herself. Someone saw her in there and busted her out. A savior found her, too.

Hades had a chip embedded under her nape. She would be found and scanned. Plus, Kori's cell phone number was on her collar for others to call. Kori knew people to call to check shelters. The woods are a square mile, a few retail stores nearby, with busy roads, and she couldn't help but imagine that last second of Hades turning to see the grill of a car crashing down.

Call someone. Call the authorities.

Authorities. Just people like you and me with uniforms. Her dad had told her that often.

She placed the girl's body in the back seat of her car, and then stared at the tree line, waiting. Still nothing. The sun was rising higher, the day getting hotter, those leading regular lives were going about their day.

She decided to drive away.

The brisk morning air rushed in through the broken window as she drove, but not enough to wake the girl laying in the back seat. Cars full of drivers fueled by a full night of sleep, freshly showered, were driving off to work, and she was returning home after being held captive in the tunnels of the hospital. Her dad still there, like she suspected, her dog now gone. Glass was sprinkled on the passenger side.

She needn't worry about carrying a body into her house in the light of day with the neighbors watching. *It won't matter,* she thought, as she pulled into the driveway. *We've been carrying so much back and forth, what's one more body?*

Let someone call the police, they would be doing her a favor, making the decision for her.

She cradled the body as if carrying a bride into their empty house, and lay the body on the hardwood floor, gently. The girl didn't look the same in the safety of her home. Her features had softened even more, her eyes less deep, skin fresher, muscles less defined, but her mouth and fingers still stained with blood. Her clothes looked days old and carried at least a few days' worth of dirt.

Dad said 'she' was coming. His 'other girl.' The one who couldn't die.

She had come, it seemed, and she had saved Kori by attacking her dad.

Should Kori go back for him?

Hell no, he wasn't alive, he wasn't breathing, and those Vrykolokas, freshly unchained, had surrounded him as she left out.

For a brief second, Kori wanted to make this girl suffer for what she did to her dad. The same anger she had towards psychiatrists and hospitals, towards pharmaceutical companies and police, towards all those who tried to help with noble intentions, but tragic results. They all deserved to be punished and feel the same hurt she had felt.

But stronger was the urge for answers and to nurse this person back to health, and Kori watched the sleeping girl in wait. She didn't want anyone else to question her when she woke, didn't want any new people with uniforms finding her dad, and she was sure that whatever happened to him in that hospital, that this girl in her house, who seemed to change from a beast to a sleeping princess, had answers.

Kori wouldn't call anyone. She would take care of this.

Kori's gut was aching in hunger, her nerves were twitching with fear. *Drink something. Eat something.* No food in the house, but the water still ran. She went to the bathroom, put her face under the faucet, turned her head, and let it stream into the side of her mouth. First one side, then the other. Her face got soaked and the wounds stung. She wiped with the side of her hand, and when she couldn't avoid it, looked at herself in the mirror.

Her skin was a new shade of paleness, a whiteness she didn't recognize. Her hair was a matted mess. The slices on both sides of her face were shades of red that seemed to be breathing and pulsating on their own. Just a soft touch of her fingertip next to the cuts brought a bit more blood coming forth, tears of red down her cheek. One slice went from below her eye to the bottom of her chin, and the other went diagonal, corner of her eye to her jawline.

Part of her liked it. Liked the burn of its hurt, and stared at the wounds as if they were alive.

Imagine the lies she'd have to tell about how she got these cuts. Imagine the scars stuck there forever. Her pitch-black hair on one side was shaved down to the scalp, on the other, it flowed down like ivy, often covering her eyes. She hoped her look made others uncomfortable and question themselves. Question her. Question everything.

She returned to the empty front room to the body.

It had moved. Not much, but the knees had bent. Her eyes were still closed and her breathing still soft. Kori sat there holding her cell phone, sure that someone would call, or if not, the silence would offer answers.

This girl is going to wake up and kill you too.

No, she wasn't a monster anymore.

Kori hated not acting. Waiting, waiting, but she knew something was about to happen, knew it as clear as she had known her dad was still in that hospital all those years.

She sat down on the hardwood floor, waiting for the body to move again, studying her face. With one fingertip, she again pulled up the on the girl's eyelid. The eyeball was less diamond, more oval, and was darting about in spastic rapid eye movement, as if the girl was stuck in restless dreams. Every second felt like the second before she woke up, and Kori just waited and watched, feeling the blood clotting and drying on her own cheek.

She hadn't slept all night, and as soon as she thought

there was no way she could, sleep grabbed her and took her under.

The hardwood floor felt soft and safe compared to the cold cement of the hospital basement, and her dreams were filled with her dad grabbing her arm. Just like the night of *the incident*, he pulled her with such might, yanking and tugging at her, but she was stuck in a wet cement tunnel and couldn't be moved, couldn't be saved. Her dad kept pulling her anyway, and wouldn't stop until the tendons on Kori's shoulder snapped in half and it hurt like hell.

Still, her dad pulled and pulled.

Noises from somewhere, and she woke up with a startle. Something she needed to see. The girl had moved again, just a bit. Her legs were curled into her chest, but she remained in her slumber.

In front of her house, a car had parked curbside. The bright sun beamed off the car fenders. *Just someone stopping to make a call*, she expected, but nope, the engine turned off, and a tall woman got out, briefcase in hand, with a stocky man alongside. They walked slowly, deliberately, pausing to investigate at her Corolla. The tall woman struggled to bend low enough to inspect inside the broken window.

Hide the body.

She quickly picked up the girl, who had grown even lighter, softer, sweeter. Kori felt like a parent carrying her child to bed, a child who had suffered in waking hours and now was in the sweet bliss of sleep. Her head rested against Kori's chest. What life had this girl had? She needed to know, but first, needed to hide her and rushed to the basement.

At the bottom of the stairs, she heard the doorbell ring.

There was an old fruit closet downstairs, dug out from the rest of the concrete, made to keep things cool from the 1950s when this house was built. A place Kori was terrified of due to the bugs inside. That was the only choice. She propped the girl up inside, closed the door, and heard the doorbell ring again.

Kori ran upstairs and opened the door. The woman stood tall and proud, as if Kori should know her, some distant family member come home after a long journey. Her arms were crossed in front of her. A plump scar rippled over her forearm. Another scar ran down her neck to somewhere below the plunging neckline. Kori waited for a badge or an announcement but there was none, just a condescending look, eyes staring down at her with pity, and the disgruntled man alongside, clearly just the sidekick.

"May we come in?"

"Um, I don't really live here. This house is no longer mine. I'm moving. No, you can't, I'm sorry."

"We can talk right here, then, but we prefer to come in. Your choice. I have so much to tell you."

"What do you want?"

"You know what. Come on, Kori. We need to talk."

She knows my name. She knows things.

"You need to see a doctor," the woman said. "Those scratches. You realize they can get infected. You never know what kind of infection can come from that. How it can change a person."

"I'm fine. I got them from a fence. Who are you? I'm kind of busy."

Kori pulled her cell out of her pocket like a weapon, as if she could dial and zap the two right out from her home.

"You look quite a bit like your father, Kori. I know your father. I know what's happening, and you have no idea what you have found. So please, invite us inside and tell us where she is."

Kori put a hand to her cheek. A wad of dried blood had puddled there while she slept, and the scratch on her leg, the one she had dismissed, had stained her jeans.

"I'm a doctor, Kori, a doctor. And I know your dad. Let's talk."

20

KORI GETS A VISIT FROM DR. ZITA

Kori invited them in, and they walked right past her, going throughout the rooms as if deciding if they should make an offer to buy. Kori was just the real estate agent, standing by, waiting for them to ask questions.

"So, this is where he had all those...*moments*," the doctor said. "God you have seen so much as his daughter. I like to think I know what you have been through, what it's been like, but of course, I can only partly know."

The woman looked at the walls as if reading invisible messages, talking to Kori but pacing about.

"You grew up revolving your life around his insanity, I know you did. His mood was your heartbeat. It wasn't *always* bad, but it *always got bad*. I heard so much about you. He did talk about you. Please know this."

He?

This doctor was inspecting the house and talking about this *He* and the assumption was the *He* was her dad. The more she talked, the more this house felt just as insane as the hospital, in much the same way, with something living underneath. Any minute, the girl in the basement was going to wake, but that didn't matter, because Kori wanted the doctor to keep talking. Just when Kori thought the secret of what happened to her dad was going to be a lifelong hidden curse, a woman with answers had walked through her front door.

When your fears reach a certain terror, there's always someone that comes to help.

The man seemed the muscle, the quiet one waiting to act once she gave the clue. He wore an untucked flannel shirt, faded jeans, boots that clearly had miles on them, and plenty of grey in his beard that had traveled just the same. His head was bald, and she could see his temples twitch when he clenched his teeth. He was all brawn, but the woman had elegance and wisdom with her grit, and the scars proof of her experience. She held a briefcase that was clearly precious to her.

It had only been a few moments, but Kori felt the doctor had already taken over her home and appointed herself ruler of the castle. Kori was the old guard in need of beheading.

"Tell me, Kori, did you see him yesterday? I know you left with *her*, but did you see *him*, too? Your father. What was he like?"

"What did you do to him? Turn him into a monster?"

"He is not a monster. I may be, for not helping him in ways I should have, but I'm here to fix that."

"Doctors never help anything much."

"You don't trust doctors, and you shouldn't. I no doubt believe you've had moments where doctors made your dad worse through mistakes. But there are no mistakes, only lessons, and lessons will be repeated until they are learned. Well, at Northville, we learned from those mistakes and created something brilliant."

The man had disappeared into the back bedrooms. *This is all wrong, the doctor was just buying time while he inspected the house.*

"See, I know you were there. The demolition company doesn't just have a fence, they now have surveillance cameras. So does Hawthorn. Took a few hours to figure things out, but I have connections. I have knowledge. And best, I have medicine. Medicine that the girl you carried out needs. This girl you have, she's sick. She's without her medicine. Let me help you both."

"What did you do to him?"

"We wanted to make him better. Kori, there is so much to say, so much to learn. I want to tell you it all. I want to tell you things that in your heart you already know to be true. But first, you tell me—do the people buying this house know about the blood on your floor?"

There was indeed blood on the floor where the young girl's body had just been. It was her dad's blood off the body of the girl.

"My face was bleeding pretty bad at first," Kori tried to

explain it away.

The man returned from the bedrooms and walked straight to the back door. He stood guard, right at the foot of the basement stairs. If the girl tried to walk up, he'd be the first to see her.

"Let me show you this briefcase," she said, and opened it as if a Rolex salesman. Inside the briefcase, at least a dozen syringes, and what looked like a gun.

"Luminex, it's called, and you can't find it in stores. Only the Luminex can save her, and..." she said, interrupting her sentence to close the briefcase. "I am the only one who has it, and it can help both her, and it can help your dad."

"My dad is dead. I saw him die."

"Ah, so you did see him. You saw something marvelous. But he may not be dead, you do not understand."

"Understand what?"

"The amazing power of regeneration his body has after it was modified. His brain can live without oxygen, his body hibernates, repairs. It happened to Lilith. *Lilith,* that is her name. She is a bit like your dad. She cycles, drastically. I need to get the Luminex into her. She may be unconscious now, but that won't always be the case between cycles. Her body will adjust. She will crave the mania, she will learn how to use it. When she wakes, she'll remember what she did. When she gets used to it, and when the moon starts to wax gibbous, she'll be back again and even more dangerous."

"So she's some fucking werewo—"

"Stop yourself from saying that!" the doctor raised her voice, pointing a finger, and gave laser eye contact for the first time. "Don't call it that, don't. It's not that. That cheapens it and there is no such thing. God, you're still just a kid and don't deserve any of this."

The doctor walked by the wall and detected the chip in the hardwood where the bullet hole from years ago was lazily filled in and caulked over, but never sanded, never painted, never fully fixed. She pushed her finger inside it as if dusting for fingerprints.

"Is this house empty? Tell me now, Kori."

"I told you we were moving," Kori said fast as she could, because she got the sense this woman would detect any lies. *What will happen when she realizes the girl is here?*

"Tell me, what did you see of her, what was she like? Did you admire what you witnessed?"

The girl had warned of a doctor.

"Look, I don't even know who you are or if you are telling me the truth? How do I know anything you say is true?"

"Truth is, you invited me in. Maybe a mistake. Truth is, I believe she's here, or nearby, but I also believe you and I working together, in union, will be so much more helpful."

"Work together for what?"

"To give you back what you love. To save both of them."

"Both of them?"

"If we do this right, you *will* see him again. If we do this wrong, this whole city, this whole state, is going to be torn apart once the walls of that place get torn open. I have what you need. The story of what happened to your father, and maybe even your dog."

Kori was in a new kid of shock.

"Oh, yes. I know about your poor dog too."

This woman was toying with her. Kori felt her anger grow and wanted to express it with force. If there was an object in the house, she would have grabbed it with both hands and tossed it at the doctor, just to get the first shot in before her ogre side-kick came to her aid. She'd done that half a dozen times as a kid, throwing things at *authorities,* and each time it felt better.

"What happened to him?" Kori demanded to know. "Stop fucking with me! Tell me what you know or get out."

"I know a lot, and I'll tell you. In exchange, you will show her to me, you will *give* her to me. There's no stopping that deal. Stop me from speaking if you wish to break that deal, but I suspect you have no choice. Of course, I'm telling you some truths that may scare you, but that's exactly what you want me to do."

21

DR. ZITA'S FIRST INTERVIEW AT NORTHVILLE PSYCHIATRIC

"I understand you like nobody else does, Kori. You and I both want the same thing. Both of us have had to tip-toe across a minefield growing up. Both of us were born to parents with an affliction we've been trying to fix all our lives, every failure we feel as personal — and there were certainly failures. The attempted fix so often makes things worse. I know that your dad was given medications that made him worse.

"I was left by my parents, even more alone than you. But I was going to find a way to *fix her*, to try something new, because it would be foolish to do the same thing again and again expecting different results. But that's what they did with my mom, and that's insanity. Same efforts, same results, and she died, *unfixable*.

"'Foolish consistency is the hobgoblin of little minds,' is what Emerson said, but adored by so many, especially psychiatrists. And I realize what else he meant when he said, "for nonconformity, the world whips you with its displeasure," for my path was not an easy one. I was going to fight those who would succumb to such hobgoblins and forge something new.

"I was recruited to work at Northville Psychiatric Hospital by the long-time medical director, Doctor William Wilson.

"He gave me a tour first, showing me the city within a city, really. Dentist office, hydrotherapy, swimming pool, bowling alley, a theater, a butcher and bake shop. Even an operating room, and a morgue when things go poorly. Rather than hospital white, sixteen shades of paint were used on the walls. Soothing music was broadcast throughout the hospital.

"It was built with suicide-proof windows when you go up to the sun deck, and bomb shelter when you go down.

"Yep, Kori, you've been trespassing inside the bomb shelter for the whole city should the country be attacked. If a nuclear apocalypse hits, those inside the hospital would survive better than anyone in the whole state. Imagine it being up to the patients inside to repopulate the world. If so, the hospital would need to create the best humans possible. That is what Dr. Wilson wanted, and how he wanted me to approach my work.

"'In psychiatry like all things, *be dangerous or be nothing*,' Wilson said to me. *Be dangerous or be nothing*, He had shared my high school yearboook quote, and I could tell this wasn't coincidence. He knew so much about me, not only my work, but my personal life.

"He believed we were all driven by our original wound, that one early imprint on our psyche that leaves a mark, and every other hurt after is just digging into the same cut. He knew about my mom. He'd read case files.

"He understood my non-traditional efforts at the community mental health center, alongside a team of social workers where I was creative. I used medications off-label. I made desperate moves to save lives. I broke boundaries. I went to homes or places in the city, visiting those in need, like I'm doing now with you. Things that no doctor would ever do.

"He wanted someone like me. He needed someone like me.

"I started the job knowing the hospital was closing on orders from Governor Engler, but Doctor Wilson always rephrased that, saying; 'we're not closing doors, not *closing doors*. We are really opening doors. *Opening doors* for the patients to leave from."

"There had been patients there for twenty years, and the hospital was tasked with getting every one of the 239 patients ready to leave — a far cry from the 2,000 they had in 1960.

"'We're *opening doors*,' Wilson kept repeating, 'and what rushes out of the open door depends on us.'"

"One last shot to make things right, and whoever was hired would be in charge of some of those transitions. My job was to help him unleash the patients onto the streets. The city was worried about the asbestos in the hallways, but they should have really been afraid of the trauma inside that was about to seep into the community.

"He needed someone to fight against convention the way I had. Someone who wouldn't destroy what these patients have, but crystalize it. 'It's the only way they will survive,' he explained. 'We can't destroy these people's gifts — then they're defenseless. We don't treat the mind, we need to unleash it. We learn the magic to make the puppet live on its own.'

"He wanted an army of patients trained to attack the world once those doors opened.

"He told me stories of successful patient, spoke on them like a proud parent. The case I remember most was of Gregor Samorski.

"Gregor was diagnosed with Major Depressive Disorder, spent time in every hospital in the area and was treated with countless medication mixes. Everything the world of psychiatry could provide. RTMS wrapped around his skull, and a dozen ECT seizures did nothing. But after he came to Northville Psychiatric, they discharged him with no medications at all.

"Doctor Wilson felt the cushion of depression probably saved this boy's life when he was young, and instead of offering medications on their first meeting, the doctor simply told him a story.

"He told the story of a boy stranded on a deserted island full of jagged rocks, sharp as glass, and a volcano that towered above the island. The boy was resilient enough to climb trees full of thorns, cutting him constantly, just to reach fruit. He had to swim for lobster and face an army of jellyfish stings. The volcano would spit molten lava that would hit and burn his skin. His flesh sizzled, forming thick, brutal blisters over the scars. He'd sit on the rocks, longing for hope, but wishing he could die, and finally decided to climb the volcano and dive into the boiling lava, praying for the relief of death."

"But death did not welcome him as he had wished, for his skin was now an armor of unburnable strength. All the cuts and burns and slices into his hide developed a scar made of armor. When the volcano got a taste of him and the spirit inside, it exploded and caused a tremendous eruption. It propelled the boy into the air, flying for thousands of miles into the middle of the sea.

"He hit the water with a puff of smoke and when the salt of the sea hit his flesh, a new species was born. A powerful, impenetrable species, super-powers born of his sickness.

"Gregor had sat fascinated at the story, realizing the story was about him, and all the while staring at the *Boplace* stationary on the doctor's desk, and when Dr. Wilson explained that Boplace was a medication in stage three of testing, and only a select few of the patients at the hospital were able to be prescribed it, Gregor pleaded his case to be chosen. Two sessions later, Gregor agreed to take the pill, two times a day, and the Boplace running through his system was the final push that changed everything. He was discharging with such excitement, and his affect was brighter than it had been in a decade.

"Boplace was nothing. Just a placebo, meant to trick Gregor's brain to use what was already inside, rewire the generations of trauma response.

"As part of the transition team to get the patients ready, Doctor Wilson needed someone like Gregor, someone who dove into the fire, because like all of them, I would be jumping into the volcano, too.

"It's important you know all this, Kori, and that he meant it. He wanted an army of patients to attack once the hospital closed. He was creating them. I'm convinced he still thought he was being noble, but he was willing to prove a point even if others were hurt. For you see, there is a small squad of soldiers inside the hospital *right now*. Your dad, in a sense, is the leader. Lilith was the best result, the most powerful, by far the most refined and most sentient.

"The rest of them? Well they were mistakes, lessons in what not to do. They are not so perfect, and those are the ones in chains."

22

DR. ZITA'S FIRST DAYS AT NORTHVILLE PSYCHIATRIC HOSPITAL

Kori shifted her weight. Her face was stinging with pain and her stomach growling with hunger. She listened to each word, and in her empty gut, felt she was being set up. She was being played. Buttons were being pushed, invisible strings were being pulled, but she couldn't cut the strings, because she needed to hear what was coming next.

"Your life changed when I was chosen to work there, Kori," the doctor explained. "I was the newest member of Northville Psychiatric and certainly the most fascinated. You've been to the buildings, you know — the place is like a drug. When you put that many people in one area with brains battling mental illness, a galaxy of synapses exploding inside each head… Well, I won't say I loved it, but I was drawn to it."

"Being out in the community, at home, at the grocery store, anywhere else felt like being away from the hive, but the real buzz of my soul was inside the hospital. It had come to accept me, but more than that, *invite* me, call to me. I slept in rooms reserved for patients more than once. I spent seventy-two straight hours at times, because leaving only made me realize how much I missed it. It was exciting, dangerous, and addictive."

Kori silently agreed, thinking of her first time in the building. It was like a huge beating heart at the middle of the earth summoning her. The mystery beckoned her day after day, and she never tired of finding new rooms, new buildings, new hallways to explore, imagining the backstories in each area. She may have been there for opposite reasons than the doctor, but a thread connected them.

And their wounds connected them.

The doctor's forearm scar was an exotic shade of pink, and that same color was about to be striped on Kori's own face once her wounds healed. The doctor moved her hands as she spoke, and the scar flashed in the air like a conductor's baton.

"It took cathedral thinking to build that hospital, creating with expansive thoughts for generations to follow," the doctor explained. "Brick and mortar eight stories high in building A, each smaller building with its own purpose, and with tunnels underneath to connect it all. It was majestic.

"Nursing staff sized me up constantly those first few days, me being the new doctor, and the patients watched me with the same interest and suspicion. I was the doctor's new disciple. The well-lit hallways were just the water Doctor Wilson walked upon. It was nothing less than Charlie being taken on a tour through the Chocolate Factory by the eccentric but brilliant Willy Wonka. The compound was his fortress. He adored it, often pausing to marvel and reflect on how it was built, as if a living organism.

"He could walk into any hallway and gauge the temperature of the patients inside, sense things in each room, a skill I worked hard to pick up. You've seen all these rooms, Kori, I know you have. We are connected that way.

"He was fond of telling me, '*My house has many rooms, and if this were not true, I would not tell you that a place is prepared for you.*'

"He was quoting John from the bible, and I knew the reference. He explained how knowing the Bible is essential, for it will help you understand the religiosity so often present in psychosis. He felt that patients speak from the collective unconscious during moments of psychosis and paranoia. That paranoia is just 'the primal mind responding to threats from past lives.' The fears may be unfounded and completely devoid of evidence in this world, but responding to some deeper meaning of another life, of human kind in general, or perhaps of their race. 'Imagine,' he said with excitement, 'the epigenetics of races with ancestral slavery or genocide in their genes, or further back in time, what our primitive minds deemed a threat, and the primal release to fight back against that threat.'

"'Someday soon I'll show you the room I've prepared for you,' he said. He meant the room where you saw your dad. He promised me I'd be on the cutting edge of genetic testing to optimize psychotropics.

"'Imagine what kind of species we can build before we open the doors of this place. What if we could genetically load certain traits, not just with the parents' DNA, but by modifying body chemistry at the very moment of procreation. What if?' he asked, but didn't want an answer. Not from me, at least, but from some higher being, waiting for moments as if he was to receive permission, and when the answer was only silence, he walked on, my feet tapping the hallways beside him.

"The doctor had some amazing perspectives on your dad's diagnosis, Kori, and trust me, I'm getting there.

"'You'll hear that Bipolar is over-diagnosed of late, but I challenge that,' the doctor said. 'What we call Bipolar Disorder is actually more present than we realize, and growing for a reason. The symptoms lie dormant for so long but are appearing at this point in history to help the human race survive. Life has its own instinct, and in order to survive it wants us to return to our most powerful state.

"Bipolar is a gift. The manic energy helps us thrive and nourish with energy unlimited, to hunt and reproduce. The depression that follows allows us to hibernate after the kill and repair and rebuild. The answer isn't curing Bipolar, but tapping into it and harnessing its strengths to become something more powerful.'

"We disparage these individuals who crave illegal drugs, not asking ourselves if the body really knows something. Does it want cocaine to release something special? Or alcohol to quench a fire that is dangerous? Can we honor what we call *illness* as a special quality instead? Bipolar-stricken individuals who don't want to take their meds are trying to do just that, to honor their gifts, but we dismiss them.

"He went on about things too esoteric to share with you, about the role of epigenetics in the transgenerational transmission of the effects of trauma, about behaviors of males and females in tribes — caretakers, hunters-gatherers — it exists in our underlying DNA. Our ancestors' neuroendocrine structure is strongly influenced by memories of trauma experience. Fears and threats experienced by earlier generations can influence the structure of our genes, making them more likely to *switch on* negative responses to stress and trauma.

"Dr. Wilson was constantly testing me, gauging me, waiting for my reaction as I sat in on interviews and he went places no other psychiatrist would. He'd wait for me to object. I never did. I watched him work with patients, preparing them for the transition program, and was learning skills of manipulation that were nothing short of magic once I was on my own.

"'Opening doors, opening doors,' he kept reminding me, 'and we need to transition the best patients, those who are willing to fully invest.' He stressed the importance of this. 'We need the patients to agree, because if they don't, if they feel they haven't signed up for the treatment and are forced, it changes the outcome. Everyone has hopes unreleased, something they're desperate for. We need to discover that, and once we do, the patients will endure any hardship. Show me what someone really wants — their gaping wounds that need fixed — and then show me what they fear — their worst nightmare — and I can get them to do anything.

"He taught me how to do what I do, and it was his teachings that lead me to interview your father. Kori, your dad *agreed* to our unique treatment for his Bipolar Disorder after I interviewed him.

"What he feared most was his daughter becoming just like him, of you being stuck in a hospital. What he hoped for most was to be with you again. And I'm telling you that can still happen."

23

KORI ASKS WHY

Kori had such urges to stop the doctor and ask questions, but didn't want to intervene and stop the momentum. She didn't want to pause the information that was gushing out this doctor's mouth who seemed so eager to purge. The strange girl hidden in her basement had warned about the doctor and pleaded, *Don't let her find me like this,* but Kori had been waiting all her life for these answers—answers she had been seeking every time she trespassed the abandoned hospital.

Kori wanted to hear it all, but each cell in her body felt delirious and weak from hunger. The cuts on her face pulsated with pain and urgency. The nerves were exposed and raw and her impatience was growing.

"Why did my dad even go there?" she finally had to ask. "He's been to so many other hospitals, why there?"

"Of all the truths you need to prepare yourself for, one that will anger you the most is this: your dad was chosen. Dr. Wilson had been researching the most extreme evidence of strength and psychosis in all of Michigan. Then they sought and found your dad in the community."

"Found him?"

"Yes. Found your dad and brought him to Northville Psychiatric."

"So, you fucking kidnapped him and then held him hostage."

"Committed him involuntarily. Any doctor who found your dad in the mental state he was in would have done a seventy-two-hour hold."

"That's a hostage."

"He saw your dad's gifts. Researched him, same way he researched and recruited me. The doctor was recruiting patients for the hospital, rather than work with those who had already been admitted, for those were failures. He wanted better subjects, because all of his efforts created something monstrous, things he kept alive for their blood. He needed better genetics, more refined symptoms, so he scoured medical files of nearby hospitals, researching them for the best sample subjects, and then seeking them out.

"Your dad remembers you, Kori, he thinks of you. Trust that. Your dad and Lilith's mom received a treatment they agreed to, motivated by the perfect carrot and a terrifying stick. You see, Kori, you were both carrot and stick. Seeing you the reward, fear of you committed to Hawthorn, the final stick.

"Your dad didn't want you shut out completely the way you were. He signed a release of information, but it was Doctor Williams who tore it up. I didn't witness it, but that's what he did. He forged and faked case files. He did what he could to find the best specimens.

"Lilith's mom was my first research project, and a magnificent specimen. I'd read about her in medical records from dozens of facilities. She'd been hospitalized many times before, sometimes months, and was genetically loaded for mental illness. Her mom had successfully suicided shortly after her birth. We looked further back and found generations of the same.

"After her dad died, she lived with the dead body for weeks until the neighbors complained and authorities visited her home. She met them with delusions that her dad was still speaking to her from the odors, and a waterfall rush of mania, of fervent religiosity. She believed she was the mother of God, at times convinced that she was pregnant with Jesus, and her manic hyper-sexuality led sex with her unscrupulous pastor. We aligned ourselves with the pastor of her church, he helped us rescue her from a life of hardship, and we brought her to the hospital.

"Like your dad, she was born with such strength. A magnificent body, the kind others beg for at a gym. I remember during my interview with her, just the exposed bit of her shoulders so supple, her long fingers often crossed over each other, each one stoking each other like crickets, like the music of the night. Her delusions revealed a larger truth, truths unspoken and unseen. Such gifts.

"She was evidence that the psychosis that comes with Bipolar is not necessarily seeing or hearing things that aren't truly there, but instead, seeing and hearing *everything that ever was there*. They detect every bit of stimulus which most of us are wired to ignore so that we aren't deluged with too much information. If you're in tune with too much, you're overwhelmed, and thus debilitated in society.

"Lilith has that. You heard it, I am certain, experienced it. In just your short time together, I bet you heard her speak to things nobody else knew of."

Kori instantly thought of her words from outside the hospital: *The Medusa Messiah*

"And your dad has such strength, a magnificent resiliency, in times of mania. We've read of some of his powers. I've never seen such restraints needed or Haldol cocktail injections more than in his case. We read the police report of the night he hurt you, and we saw the divorce proceedings. He was immune to the taser at the height of his mania. Pain actually makes his body stronger, more energized, and the bullet wound likely did nothing. In that way, these two were the perfect mates."

"So, this girl. The one you are looking for…what is she like?" Kori asked, wondering what the girl might do if she awoke in the basement and came shooting up the stairs.

"She is a perfect combination of mental acuity, spiritual awareness, and physical strength. My hypothesis is that Lilith will be able to use all the stimulus she soaks in and use it for her own power. Rather than fear it, she will *ask it all to come into her.* Welcome it. She will not be handcuffed by such as a curse, but be elevated by the gifts into something near-Godly. And her offspring?" The doctor paused, place her hand on her stomach, just above her waist. "Well, Lilith's offspring will be even more powerful."

Kori had a hard time seeing the unconscious girl in her

basement do such things, but then remembered the flurry of power she witnessed in the hospital.

"And as you have guessed, this fantastic young girl is related to you. This one you think you're protecting—she is your half-sister. Lilith's mom is looking for her too.

"You see, her mom is out there, and it won't take long for her to show up and try to reclaim her cherished daughter she lost so many years ago."

24

KORI LEARNS OF THE BIRTH

"*My house has many rooms,* is what Doctor Williams said quite often. Tell me Kori, do you know what that means? A question I ask and will answer myself, which is what Doctor William Wilson himself did quite often.

"He spoke about his many rooms before finally bringing me down to the transition area in the hospital tunnels. This was the safest place for such events. The secrecy required it. The atmosphere all changed from medical to industrial, no longer the soothing paint and cleanliness of above, no more music piped in, but there was a barren coldness there—cement, metal.

"The rooms were built as an add-on, for everyone's safety, and treatment was administered by air vents, by mouth, by injection, or by IVs. We watched it all from afar. All of it was being recorded.

"Your dad has no doubt had medication that made him worse. It's a travesty of pharmaceuticals that patients seeking treatment are actually agitated and triggered into acute mania when doctors gave them an anti-depressant rather than a mood stabilizer. It just makes Bipolar worse.

"Well, Doctor Wilson wouldn't agree with *worse,* he would say sharper, and he used an amalgam of activating anti-depressants, steroids, and his own concoction of methamphetamines—the purest of stimulant from a cocoa plant, cooked and crystalized right in the tunnels."

"Each new patient failure brought about changes, not just in chemical make-up, but in timing. Finding the best time to inject was a struggle. It mattered. It needs to match the natural rhythm of the Bipolar mood shifts and the pull of the closest power that changes the tides, pulls at our souls and pulls at our psyches—the moon.

"Yes, the moon. Endogenous rhythms of circalunar

periodicity and their underlying genetic basis is part of who we are. It's part of our bipolar heritage.

"Humans were meant to hunt by the light of the moon. Multivariate lunar-associated pathways change electromagnetic fields, they augment the Earth's magnetosphere, signaling it's time to wake and hunt. The reflected sun off the celestial rock lights up your prey, stops them from hiding, and during this illumination those who did not sleep, those with the most acute senses, were the ones who flourished. That is why mania survives to this day.

"Bipolar is something from our shadow shelves, our primal selves, pulled out of us when the time is right and the full moon shines. The boundless energy, the grandiose confidence, primal passions, acute senses, and savage strength get triggered. Hyper-sexuality kept the population of primitive man booming, straight up fucking like mad and hunting for nourishment.

"Can you imagine a tribe of humans full of mania? How amazing they would be?

"Not just aggression, but perception, those who could sense and anticipate the feelings, thoughts and movements of the enemies around them. Those who survived knew how to protect themselves by knowing their enemies, sensing their threats, hearing the bell before it rings.

"Wilson bred them, put them together in the same room, chemically manipulating their mania at just the right times, knowing that with extreme hyper-sexuality, that procreation would happen at the height of fertility, both mother and father already turned into something godlike.

"And each time we procreated — each time they procreated — we took blood from the newborn, made into palette-rich plasma, and injected it into the mom as part of our barrage of chemicals. We kept creating an exponentially more enriched elixir. It stirred something so primal, something dormant, the amazing amount of emotional reactivity and memory in the prefrontal cortex. Neural orbs are enlarged, and the pituitary gland releases adrenal hormones in the blood stream, epinephrine and cortisol levels beyond what humans should be able to tolerate.

"The first time I saw some of the video tapes of newborns taken from their mothers, I was nauseous, and if I had to do it again, I would have run right to the Michigan licensing board. I rationalized that in a few ways. The board was hardly monitoring, for they knew the facility was closing on edict from the governor. And a pregnancy in a long-term facility was not unheard of. You can't have a thousand people in a building and stop sexual activity and conception.

"Doctor Wilson knew I would keep quiet. He knew I would be amazed by the brilliant pharmacology mix and the stages of testing. Some of the infants, the products before Lilith, were not nearly as refined. Born with deformity, he kept them alive, and always at each step of the way perfecting a mood sedative he called Luminex. A gift, the life-saving Luminex. A trace of Lithium inside, some refined benzos, some silver salts, a touch of Ketamine."

Doctor Zita gave a pat to her briefcase, while her sidekick stood guard with arms crossed, still standing by the basement steps.

No sign of the hidden girl in the fruit cellar below.

"Wilson had been saving the children who were born before I was even hired, keeping them locked, afraid of their strength. They were ferocious in cycles, aggressive and savage, and with a certain kind of intelligence. Not *smarts*, but instinct beyond anything humans could measure, incredible sensory sensitivity.

"He was creating life because he could, genetically mutating. Refining the gifts already present through their life of mental illness. He was playing out his own Frankenstein story. He kept them alive and fed them, certain that meant they would treat him like a grateful dog to its owner. Instead, they attacked and ate him alive first chance they could. Good thing those chains they're in are now nearly unbreakable.

"Killed by his own creation," Zita said, shaking her head. "It was messy, ugly, and a bit pathetic. Something I will never let happen. His death was explained away. Wilson had no family to ask questions, and I continued where he left off. I only wanted to fix the condition, not make a dozen new beings, but simply one. Just one. And then make them part of me.

"This may disgust you to hear, but I watched your dad and his mate conceive on live video camera. Your dad was one of the few even strong enough to survive sexual intercourse with Maya, and the two bonded, like a pack in the wild. This hadn't happened before. Their gestation period was only fifty-nine days, similar to that of many other mammals, and exactly that of wolves.

"After she gave birth, we let her breastfeed, but once their mood dipped, we planned to add a sedative into the air and enter the room to take the child, as was the routine. We wanted her blood, to make platelet-rich serum, and most of all, I wanted the child to grow to adolescence and then harvest her eggs.

"Your dad and his mate, they were sharper than anything that came before. They could read feelings and thoughts, sense things. Your dad decided to kill the child, a mercy killing, he no doubt believed, or perhaps he wanted to force our hand, to make us open the door. We had to enter early to save the infant, we had not sedated them, but instead rushed the room armed with Luminex.

She smiled, looking over her scars. "I was wounded terribly in this attack, but we got out with the child—a child who would have been killed had I not entered. That was my last day at Northville Psychiatric. Maya escaped, but your dad was stuck for another year. I can't imagine what he went through, his deep depression and then the manic periods where he had nobody. It was beyond anything any human should ever suffer through.

"When the place closed and the power to the tunnels was cut altogether, the electronic door locks opened and your dad was set free—but he stayed there, living with those terrible beings Doctor Wilson created.

"I needed to leave with the child. I knew the mom would follow. After letting her say goodbye to the baby—I am no monster. I have the kind of warmth that comes from witnessing perpetual hurt and suffering—I bathed us both in tomato sauce and scrubbed in vinegar to dull our scents. I had an abundant supply of Luminex, and the greatest being ever born. I wrapped her in an air-tight coffin with an oxygen mask.

"I went west to California. Home schooled her some, and worked some contractual jobs for short stints…cash pay, court-ordered psych testing. Never on the books, never paid taxes. I made money then traveled. I wrote prescriptions for opioid and benzo addicts. I was creative, and made enough cash to bribe the demolition company, and to pay for the in vitro fertilization.

"I dropped my guard on the way back here. Lilith got away. In some ways, I will always cherish that vision of her… standing in the motel doorway in such glory, goddess-like. You can't fathom the girl you found. She can *smell* thoughts, *hear* colors, and has fantastic strength, summoned straight from souls all around her. And you need to understand, her mother will be here soon. Your father may as well. Those beasts? If someone lets them out...

Doctor Zita finally stopped.

"They have a savage sense of who their enemies are, who has hurt them, and this means that Lilith's mom went to avenge those who betrayed her. The Word of Faith murders? You have likely heard of them. That's Maya's masterpiece.

"I have friends in the demolition business. I know when they're starting. It's been planned. I'm here to try to protect us from those who are still inside. We traveled here for the demolition, to make sure it is complete. Those things will likely not die even when they are buried. They'll stay stuck and suffer under the rubble, fully conscious, because the brain matter persists, even if it slows, it regenerates and begins again.

"We can't let them escape for they will certainly cause apocalyptic travesty to the city. And we can't let Lilith continue on without her medication. I will care for her every moment she's alive, and that's the truth.

"Now you need to tell me where she is. Tell me now. If so, I will try to help your dad and bring him to you. If not, your dad will be buried alive with those monstrosities in the hospital basement."

25

KORI RESPONDS

Scars were stuck on the doctor's body like barnacles to a boat. They were like some sort of foreign mollusk attached to the hull, evidence of her travels through exotic territories.

The doctor knew how to talk. Her words tugged at Kori's spine, massaging her thoughts. It was a bedtime story that seduced her into a sleepy stupor.

She'd confess everything, confess it all.

She's in the basement.

Stubborn outrage returned to its rightful spot. The scratches across Kori's face seemed to be responding as well. *This story rang true*, it felt true, but not the intentions, those were hidden. A lot was hidden. Kori feared any pause in responding to the doctor's commands revealed more than she wanted, as if she was searching for what lie to say. She needed to answer.

"I can't help you," Kori said.

William Wilson, she thought, the doppelganger. My dad knew Poe, he recited passages.

Doctor Zita changed her posture, changed her very skin color, it seemed, and things shifted. "It's unfortunate that you aren't agreeing," she said. "Your dog will die, your dad will die. Both will suffer. Let's check around this house a little further, shall we?" she said, and gave a nod to the club-armed man.

There was nowhere else to check further, except the basement, and the big man started walking down the stairs, his footsteps banging loudly on Kori's brain as if he were descending down her skull.

This was about to blow up. No doubt he'd open the fruit cellar door, pull the string on the single light bulb, and he'd see the girl lying there in the light, maybe half asleep, maybe unconscious, and was about to bring her upstairs. Kori's only hope would be if she escaped out the egress somehow. Off to find her mom.

"Kori, what you need to understand is that those wicked cuts on your face…well, if you got those where I suspect, you may find yourself turning. You may even like how it feels, no doubt. I had an immediate alcohol and iodine cleanse after my wounds, and then a full blood transfusion, to stop me from being infected. But you are soiled and being penetrated with the new plasma, right now. The results shall be interesting. You'll certainly not have the power of Lilith, for she is a spectacular specimen crafted with delicacy, but next time the moon rises, you will find out how deep it has infiltrated. You will see why your dad needs to die. And if it does infect your bloodstream, we'll be coming for you."

The banging from the steps returned. Kori heard the man's feet coming up the stairs, each boom getting louder, until he reached the top. She didn't even turn to look, feigning as if there was nothing to see, but she could tell by the pounding of his steps he was carrying weight up the stairs.

The weight of Lilith.

The doctor's eyes lit up. Kori turned to see the man holding the body of Lilith, her eyes closed. The coma continued.

The doctor shook her head towards Kori, a schoolteacher shaming a five-year-old.

"The demolition will start in two weeks, well before the next moon. You know why? The next one is a super blood moon. You don't want to see what happens under the red skies of a blood moon. I have pity on you, please know that I do, and just to prove it is so, I will leave you one of these."

The doctor reached in her briefcase, and handed Kori a syringe.

"Use this if things start feeling…*unusual*, for you, or should you choose to go visit your dad. Intracardiac injection, right into the heart will cause death, but intramuscular injection will sedate the mania when the full moon rises. I've been using it for years to stop Lilith from changing. Soon, a shot into her heart will stop the beating altogether, but her godly offspring lives inside me. If you don't want your dad buried alive for eternity, I suggest you remember what I said. Maybe go there soon, before the demolition."

The doctor was doing her own confession, disclosing that her first pitch to Kori had been lies. Her true intentions revealed, she left with Lilith out the front door. Kori watched them drive away, and the noise in the house escalated, the silence and loneliness, haunting her in symphony. Her first urge was to move, get back to the hospital and convince her dad to leave, but she instead did nothing, waiting as if someone was supposed to tell her what to do. All she could hear was the house breathing, speaking, whispering to her, but in words of a foreign language or some forgotten tongue. Everything swirled around her head until the roof was about to cave in, leaving her trapped inside, but stuck alive.

That's what ghosts are, right? Trapped but can't ever leave.

The girl Lilith was younger than her, a sister, or half-sister, and she had known the doctor was going to come for her, but Kori couldn't keep her safe. Same with Hades.

Enough contemplation. She rose to her feet and walked out the front door.

The smashed-in windshield reminded her this wasn't just a dream, this was real. Pieces of shimmering sharp pieces were still stuck to the seat. Hades might be cut, wherever she is.

She drove to a Wendy's drive-thru, ordered a single with cheese, large fries, and a Coke, and ate it as she drove. Sauce dripped on her shirt that she wiped off with a French fry while waiting at stop lights. Every bit of fat filled her empty parts, and she ate the burger in five bites, chasing it down with the Coke and more fries. The grease got on her cheek and the slashes on her face stung in response.

She swore she could hear a noise emanating from the wounds.

She leaned over to take quick looks at the mirror. The cuts were turning all shades of red, and she had purple rainbow bruises on her neck from where the guard had strangled her.

God, she looked like hell when she walked into Target, wearing the same dirty clothes, gaping wounds still seeping, while everyone else was going about their day.

Maybe she'd always looked like this, it was just nobody could see.

More than one person's eyes got wide and stared at her as she filled up a small basket. She bought three huge water bottles, a set of butcher knives, a twelve-pack of Snickers bars, and a flashlight with batteries included. She was going to blow the place up in light and chop up what needed chopping.

She drove with backpack in the passenger seat and parked at Hawthorn, far away as she could from activity, but there were still too many cars, too many people, and too much daylight. She imagined the lives of those parked here and felt a mix of anger and pity. Visiting their children at the facility, patients stuck in that purgatory of waiting for their return home from Hawthorn. She imagined the trepidation of what comes next, the expected demise when things go poorly, and then the foolish consistency of taking them back to the same place who failed to help them.

That's what she's been—just one of an army of hobgoblins terrorizing her dad, trying to fix things with foolish consistency, over and over again, repeating the same efforts that didn't work.

She got out of her car hoping Hades would sense her presence and come sprinting to her, but nothing. She was alone.

She trampled through the Evil Woods, imagining animals and creatures in the woods, possums, deer, bugbears and tree imps, all taking notice, bearing witness to her journey. She ventured past them all, looking for Hades along the way. The dog would follow scents, she knew that for certain, but in this place unknown, where would they lead?

The fence itself was gaping open more than before, no need to even bend the metal back anymore, just a short duck to walk right by. She passed through, just another creature of the Evil Woods now, walking through the gates of Hell, clinging to hope as she entered.

The demolition equipment towered like dirty metal Tonka toy trucks in front of Northville Psychiatric. Workers were moving among the trucks, so she moved along the edge of the woods, waiting until she'd be shielded by the brick building, and then dashed across the open land, backpack bouncing against her shoulder blades until she reached the building. Panting, moving with her back against the wall, she snuck to her favorite entrance and made it inside. Unnoticed.

The air felt more alive and awake during the day. Light seeped through the fractures in the brick, making particles floating in the air spin with more energy, the walls humming aloud. The whispers greeted her with a surprise unheard during years of past visits.

Who is this intruder? Ah, it's you! The daughter. We've never seen you at this hour. The father is still here. Please join him.

She walked the same path she had days before, descending to the dark tunnels down the iron rungs this time, wanting to speak her dad's name and expecting him to answer.

The flashlight beam was a disinfecting light on the tunnel walls. Each surface she pointed at awakened, eyelids made of dust opening, as if pupils inside were watching her. The building was alive, breathing, the rattly lungs of a man who knew his death was coming soon. Big pipes meant to circulate the heat and blood through this massive city seemed to have thinned from aging, tired of their work, sad over their lost purpose. The floor was moist, as if a river ran at her feet. Empty chairs still sat randomly in the hall, sounds from twenty years ago still present, buried alive in these tunnels.

Her footsteps from the land above walked through it all.

She had a backpack this time. She had butcher knives. She had a syringe full of Luminex. She had water. But what she did not have was certainty of what she would do when she found her dad—dead or alive.

She certainly anticipated the moment as she marched down the hallway, but the moment was delayed, since she could not locate the hidden hallway she'd stumbled upon nights ago. It all looked different at this time of day, in the shine of a flashlight. She wanted to retrace her steps and stand in the same way she was when the guard showed up and gave chase.

It was like the portal only appeared when she was in

crisis.

She recognized the line of pipes: one large thick one, a few smaller ones alongside. Or maybe there had been none at all? How far had she run when chased? She'd walked by the rusty green file cabinet, noticed the same plastic chair — but this time the chair was standing.

Perhaps it was all just imagined, a mirage she wanted to see because she was afraid to go to Florida and be with her mom. Punishment for refusing to go, for lying to her saying, "*I'll see you soon.*"

She finally sat on the floor, back against the wall, butt cheeks on the hard cement. Occasionally, she heard a noise to the left, then to the right, and would shine the light in either direction, but nothing.

She opened her backpack and drank just a sip of water, turned the flashlight off, and stayed still. How could her dad have stayed here so long?

Before the day he had hurt her, he had been getting worse. His mood swings were shifting to more furious heights and terrible lows, and so many mornings he didn't leave the house to work, or he returned home well before school let out because the students *needed to hear a new message.* More than once, he was put on medical leave, and meetings with the union followed.

Dad finally stopped his foolish consistency of doing the same thing over and over again — this time by leaving his job, leaving his family, and staying away for good. But Kori would have preferred a sick dad over an absent dad. Mom's life had cocooned into something new, while Kori had been stuck on quests underground, looking for answers.

"He cut our souls in two, and now we're always searching for our other half — that's Zeus," her dad had said.

There was always some truth in his nonsense, if you just listened. She could still feel the worst of his suffering when he had grabbed her arm that night and yanked on her with such strength. She dreamt of that moment a hundred times since, usually Dad trying to pull her to safety, but never once succeeding, and the dream ends before both of them give up.

Kori stood to her feet to keep looking, retracing places she wasn't sure she'd been. She closed her eyes and tried to feel her way, imagined it was darker like the nights before, and only the lantern glow, like a chunk of the moon, was brought inside. Just imagining the moon and she could feel it tug at her, making her blood vessels throb as if dancing, the cuts on her face a strobe light to the music's beat.

Her finger traced the cement wall, seamlessly moving along the rough and rugged texture, nearly caressing it, until finally, a break in the wall. Just a tiny bit, something she'd not have seen with her eyes opened, and she stopped.

No handle here, just a swinging door to be pushed open. Even in this forgotten hell, there were darker corners where worse things happened.

This was it. She walked through, this time slow and deliberate.

Each step was a slight descent, a barely noticeable downhill, pulling her along the path. A couple of quick turns, left then right, and finally the hallway opened up. She came upon a larger room, just outside where her dad had held her—one that she hadn't noticed days before.

The flashlight shined upon an old computer monitor on a large conference table, clearly not seen as valuable enough to take when the hospital closed. This room likely hadn't been part of the evacuation plan. The forgotten, hidden parts of this city.

This is where the doctors observed what was happening inside.

She expected to hear movement, to be assaulted or chased, or greeted by someone—but instead it was silent. The dust hung still in the air, the only movement was her heart beating and her lungs filling with air.

Two doorways before her.

Two rooms. She had just escaped the one on the right, and she tried to prepare herself for going back inside, but instead chose diversion, and pushed open the door on the left.

Inside, and each time the flashlight beamed towards a new area, she expected to see a face, lying on the ground, frightened and frozen and been there for years. Instead it was empty and vacated. Rusty bed frames were in the corners, IV stands alongside.

This is where the girl was born.

She flashed lights on the wall and revealed what seemed like prehistoric cave drawings, drawn all in red. The painting was of trees with branches reaching to the sun, and roots spreading down into the earth. *As above, so below* was written in cursive next to it, followed by a series of sentences soaked into the concrete, faded and indecipherable.

Her dad's drawings, her dad's words, perhaps, when he'd been trapped here while she had been going about her life. When he was set free and the locks gave way, he didn't go far. He went next door to take care of the beasts, the 'mistakes,' as the doctor said. Dad was dedicated to them in a way he was never dedicated to her.

In that way, she was envious of the sickly creatures.

She put a hand over the wound on her face. It was moist, seeping, throbbing like some tracking beacon device that knew it was near its desired target.

She grabbed her cell—no service down here, of course, but she felt the screen summoning her to go to Florida and leave the haunted memories behind. Her mom was there, standing alongside her new stepdad, both of them under the scorching bright sun. Always sunny in Florida, a moonless place. Mom had blocked her first husband out in a perpetual eclipse.

But she wasn't carrying a chunk of dad's DNA like Kori was.

She finally heard a noise, the brief rustling of chains, just for a moment, and then it stopped.

Come on Kori, what are you waiting for?

She couldn't avoid it any longer, and needed to go next door, just like her dad over a dozen years ago.

She walked back to the hallway, faced the door on the right, pushed it open, and shined the flashlight.

A mass of bodies were at the center of the room in one pile. The creatures were sleeping on each other, warmed by body heat. The chains had been torn from the walls but their necks were still wrapped in the collars. They lay upon the discarded metal as if a pile of hay.

The Vrykolakas, her dad had called them, and they were like a pack of wild dogs on top of each other in a circle. Their faces with eyes closed had a sweetness to them, a fragility that contrasted to their savagery from days before. They had limbs that didn't match, arms and legs without symmetry. Their skin was leathery like that of a pig, with a pinkish hue. Some had fangs that couldn't be contained by their lips, and pierced through. A few had digits missing on their hands. All of them skinny. *It must hurt to have bodies like that*, she thought, and imagined each one of them waking up. Now that they were unchained, the danger hung thick like a stench in the room.

She moved the flashlight about the room, until—eye contact.

One was awake with eye opened.

Kori braced herself, waiting for it to sound the alarm and wake the others, but as the seconds ticked on, she realized it was sleeping as well. The pupil did not move. Its face was deformed with an eyelid that couldn't close over the bulge of its pupil, so it lived with its eyes always open. God, she felt the need to poke that eye out.

And there, cuddled in the middle of the mass, was her dad.

Dad was alive—his body was all torn up, but his chest was moving. He was breathing

He was alive.

His beard was overgrown, his skin darkened with grime, and his face looked so sad. It no longer had the primordial grimace. His eyes less sunk, his muscles sleek but not savage. The metallic scent was gone, leaving only a noxious humidity hovering in the air like a fog, and Kori saw why. The body of the guard was there, pushed to the side. Its rib cage was opened up and remained there like leftovers at a Ram's Horn.

And then two more eyes did open. Not the beasts' or her dad's eyes, but her dog's eyes. Hades.

Hades is here. Her paws moved up and down in excitement like they did whenever Kori approached and her joy got to be too much. She licked her lips, then finally trotted over, clanking on top of the discarded chains. Kori bent down to give a hug and scratches and tiny words of joy.

"Hades," she whispered, "Hades, I found you."

Words she wanted to hear from her dad. Hades had followed the scent, found a passage below, and returned. *There you go, Dad, the hero's welcome home.*

Kori kept the flashlight beam away from the eyes of the creatures, one hand scratching Hades' mane. The Vrykolakas stayed in their deep sleep, each lung on its own course, a series of inhales and exhales, in and out, and their breath stank of the decay inside their guts. She felt pity for them, but they would certainly not offer the same.

Finally, her dad seemed to sense a presence, and was the only one to awaken, stirring like some dragon whose slumber was disrupted, slowly opening up an eyelid, searching for that which had invaded its lair.

It's me. Your daughter. I'm back.

"You shouldn't be here," he whispered.

"I'm here anyway."

"But you shouldn't be. It's safe now, but won't be for long."

One of the beasts had its arms over Dad's legs. He was so wrapped up in their bodies, they were all just smaller parts of a larger being. Like Zeus had to tear them apart.

Dad rolled slightly to one side, scooting over limbs, moshing down bodies, and then got to his feet. His bones appeared to be put together differently, and he walked disjointedly to her side. Such hurt in his eyes now, rage replaced by sadness. The flurry of energy whirling about him was nowhere to be found. He was like some Bugs Bunny-Tasmanian Devil now turned Elmer Fudd. She hated seeing him like this.

He needs a hospital, she thought again and again, and then she remembered — *he came to a hospital, and this is what happened.* Her weight felt unsteady in his presence. Part of her was pulled to the exit, the other part pulled to be closer to him.

"Worry not. I'm okay now, but it won't stay like this. That's what happens. You shouldn't be here."

"Dad. We can figure this out. Your doctor. She came for me. She's about to bury you in here."

"Maybe then you can leave me and move on — I'm sorry," he said in his voice of remorse he used when his depression hit. A hopeless tone, a helpless pitch.

"No. I want you to walk out of here with me. Like *go*…go somewhere else with me. Anywhere. You need a real hospital." She realized what she sounded like. Just another hobgoblin.

"This is my last stop. I can die like this. I really can. This is where I always wanted to be," Dad pleaded. "Taking care of living things, taking care of these beasts. They're always craving and hungry, biting and nipping at me, and feeding them was easy. Each time I brought them something to eat I could feel their bellies and twisted souls get full. But feeding *you* what you needed — not so easy. So I left. But now, I'm tired. I'm ready to go."

She looked them over, knowing that not one of them were from his blood. The first creations from Doctor Wilson's breeding, the discards of patients' suffering, tossed away in this underworld hell, with her dad as their caretaker.

"It's been the life I wanted, having them look up to me, feeding from my hands. I knew how to care for them. Much as I tried with you, much as I tried with each of my students, I failed. 'Nothing to offer but my own confusion' — *that's Jack*," he said, another quote. "Now that they're unchained, I suspect I'll learn they don't love me. When the moon shines again, all of us will turn, and they'll attack me. It's in their nature, and I won't win that fight without chains to hold them back."

"So leave here with me. Let's go find help."

"There is no help out there above. Only one thing can help me, and she gave it to you."

Kori shrugged her arms in confusion.

"The silver. She gave it to you, and you brought it."

"The silver?"

"The silver, the Luminex. I can tell you have it on you. I feel it in the room. Doctor Z hit me with it the day everything blew up. I will never forget it. I can still remember how it felt."

She dug the syringe out from her backpack.

"She's beguiling, that doctor," her dad warned. "She lies and manipulates with truths you want to hear."

"And she's tearing this place down, Dad. She said you might not die but would just be stuck here."

"She told you how the silver will fix me, right?"

"No, she said just temporary. And you don't like to take medicine, I know that. You need a doctor, a regular doctor."

"You know well as I do it's beyond that now. And you know by *fixed* I mean put to sleep for good."

His speech seemed covered in a thick scent, like resin from the decaying hospital and the breath of these tiny monsters had clung to them. Every single word was covered thicker than the one before. Each moment in time forward, just a little bit worse.

"I'm not going to kill you. I'll help you. I'm not some murderer or assassin."

"You're neither. 'You're an errand boy, sent by grocery clerks, to collect a bill'– *that's Apocalypse Now*, and I'm your Kurtz"

Kori kept staring into his sad, glassy eyes, wanting to turn away, but realizing this was likely her last look.

"The infection, it grows. It really does. People like Maya, people like me, we won't give it to anyone, we wouldn't want anyone to catch this from us. She visited me once. I disgust her, and rightly so. You can put me down, Kori. You can and should. Some of the best heroes in the world have put their fathers down. It's how it works. You can put an end to it. The doctor told you how."

"You won't come home with me? I want you to live, not die."

"My Kori, forbid me now to die? Don't deny me death, it's not hurting anything."

His flesh was full of so many cuts, each of them like

zippers, loose zippers, ready to break and let the insides spill out.

He wouldn't survive on the surface anymore.

She'd been in this moment all her life, trying to save Dad, trying to rescue him from his little monsters and eternal demons. And here she was trying to do the same thing. *Foolish consistency is the hobgoblin of little minds*, and that's what she was. She was more hobgoblin than anything in the room.

Kori had watched a handful of dogs be euthanized. She had felt the life leave the body of an animal put to sleep. It was all part of her training. *You should see what it's like.* Watching an animal put to sleep was easier than she thought, fully peaceful. What wasn't peaceful was the body afterwards, as if it was then stuck in perpetual suffering.

"You should have left me to die," her dad had said after his suicide attempt. *"You didn't need to call for help so fast. You made a mistake. Ain't no use, living this life in conditions like mine."*

This was her chance to shatter the foolish consistency and do something different instead of repeating past failures. It would open up a new kind of future. Move on to Florida, or better yet, any state, knowing her dad slept and rested in peace and all because she had the courage to do as he asked.

"I'm going to lay down and close my eyes," Dad said. "Imagine us somewhere else, in the sun, at home baking, maybe a garden, not here. Only you can put me there permanently."

A thousand possibilities went through Kori's head. None of them made any more sense than doing what he asked, no carrot held any hope. The fear of leaving her dad down here to be buried alive terrified her enough to move her hand.

She held the needle up over her dad's chest. He lay on the ground waiting for the relief a slam into his heart from the Luminex would bring. Both her hands were wrapped in fists around the syringe ready to plunge.

Intracardiac injection will cause death.

"You probably have to slam it hard, Kori."

Stop being his hobgoblin of foolish consistency.

Her fingers trembled like a dying Pope's, offering his last communion to a desperate Catholic. She took a few breaths, looking for courage and wisdom. She wanted the building to tell her what to do, to make the decision for her, but nothing. She clenched her fingers tighter, partly hoping the syringe would snap in half, Luminex gone and spilled on the ground. Decision made.

I can't do this. I can't.

This wasn't courage, this was fear and cowardice and running. So much easier to put him to death, then to move on. *Real courage*, true courage would be to join him. To live and die right here along with him until the place collapsed over her.

She put the needle down to her side, and in that moment, felt a relief she'd not had in a dozen years, but soon as she did, her dad cupped her hand and lifted it back up. The skin on his hand so rough. This wasn't him anymore—his hands couldn't bake, couldn't strum a guitar, couldn't hold hers the way a father should. Somewhere beneath the grime of his illness there remained something beautiful, but it had already been buried too deep.

She felt just as lifeless as he did.

Dad tugged the syringe out from her palms and held it high over his chest, like a hari-kari sword, lined it up to his heart, and without pause, plunged it inside. The horror of it all spread across his face, first in a painful grimace, but then a content smile. Like a child who'd been crying in the night finally soothed and settling in, a softness in the cement. His eyes closed to the painful sights of this dungeon, and then opened to angels within.

She indeed felt an angel watching, as if they it were entering this hell for the first time, harrowing to save the souls that were worthy.

"You are loved," her dad whispered.

Kori left his last words hang in the air long as she could, and when they faded, she plucked the syringe from his chest, tugging at it like a dart out of a dartboard.

As soon as the syringe released, it seemed to set forth a trap.

The building itself started to shake, to roar, either in agreement with his death, or in an angry objection, the walls trembled. Dust from the ceiling dropped in little raindrops of soot. Each time the thunderous noise happened, she thought it was the last, but then another, and another followed, shaking the room. Shaking her core.

Hades stood and moved about, sensing something she could not communicate fully, but the message was clear.

This was no earthquake.

The demolition was starting.

The doctor had lied. Demolition wasn't starting in two weeks. It was starting today, and Doctor Zita knew Kori would be here.

The monsters stirred, but didn't wake. Wouldn't wake. Not yet.

Her dad deserved a proper burial in a cemetery, but he would never get there. He also deserved a life and a mind that wasn't destroyed by good intentions but bad results. But that wouldn't happen, not in this timeline.

She folded his hands over his chest, once again wiped the oozing fluid off the wound on her cheek, and placed it upon his scaled lips. The fluid dapped there, on his lips, then seeped into his mouth, down deeper into his body. As above, so below. Traces of her would be inside him forever.

She flung the backpack on her shoulder, and dashed for the hallways, hoping she could get to the surface. Hades followed alongside, leaving her dad there with the beasts he'd been fighting all his life, but a sleep he'd never had. No longer would he waken with mania, with mood shifts, with this monstrous transition they forced upon him. This was the end of their efforts.

She remembered what Doctor Zita told her: "*What he feared most was you becoming like him, being stuck in a hospital.*"

And if she didn't move fast enough, his fears would come true, for the building kept roaring and shaking, louder and louder, about to be blown over and the roots yanked from the ground. As if the world said *enough of this mistreatment.*

Kori ran, and Hades ran with her, through the skinny hallway, ascending to the main tunnel, taking a quick left.

There was more than one way out, but she checked the way she entered first, moving quickly, her backpack bouncing against her spine, flashlight straining to penetrate the growing dust up ahead. Every minute another jarring noise, like thunderclaps from a storm getting closer.

A dust cloud from soot blocked her path, so she stumbled through it, hand over mouth, coughing out tiny bits of the building from her lungs, until finally she came upon a mound of concrete. The tunnel was completely blocked.

They started with this area on purpose. The doctor knew she'd come here, maybe even watched her.

The tunnels went to other buildings. She knew this. There were other ways out, rungs up to manhole covers that she'd not yet explored.

Hades was terrified, alert, but just as confused.

If they didn't find a safe passageway to the surface, they both would be buried alongside the sleeping Vrykolakas, who were sure to wake up when the blood moon rose.

26

MAYA AT HOME

The sun was setting and dusk approaching. One lone child rode his Big Wheel on the sidewalk, desperate to get a few more laps in before the street lights came on and his dad called him inside for good. His knees bobbed up and down with eager enthusiasm, plastic tires bouncing over sidewalk cracks. His arms clutched the steering wheel, and the black plastic tires burned onto the pavement when he skid to a stop.

Then he turned around and did it all over again.

The sound drifted up to the second story of the abandoned home, through the busted-out window to where Maya slept in her childhood bedroom. She was alone, as always, not of the world, inside this barren house, this street where the decay fought a perpetual battle against hope.

Maya was outside of it all, not of the human race anymore.

She slept days at a time, barely ate, waking up to the sun rising and shining through the window frames, or the noise of a garbage truck, or a child riding his Big Wheel on the street. She could tell where the planet was in the galaxy by her mood, she could feel the rotations of the earth spinning on its axis.

So often she curled back up into a protective ball in some corner of the house to sleep. coma-like, sometimes in the basement, sometimes upstairs. Other times she stayed awake to walk the streets, unnoticed by most.

Maya's depressive state lasted until the waxing gibbous moon shined bright enough in the sky, and for those three days she lived a lifetime.

After the depression seeped out her body and the mania flooded in to take its place, she woke with a tremendous roar. Quad muscles in her thighs bulging, biceps with magnificent new strengths, obliques in her back expanding like wings, her back hunched under the weight. The color of her eyes sizzled with new flecks of oranges and yellows rather than the browns of before. Her brow grew deeper, her gaze detecting the slightest movement, her nose sensing the spectrum of scents, her ears hearing the noise of spiders weaving their webs.

She loved to step onto the roof and feel the power of the moonlight glow. Like a plant growing to the sun, she leaned into the moonshine and bathed in its power. Creatures on the street dashed for safety—squirrels raced for trees, birds stopped their chirping and took off in flocks in the sky, bats of the night no longer fluttered, and the crickets stopped their song—all out of respect, for the queen of the land had emerged. This was her time, and her one goal was to find her child.

The Daughter is greater than the Mother, with powers more vast.

Maya moved through the streets hoping to hear the sound of her child's heartbeat, the boom that sounded like the underwater beating of drums. Or she hoped to catch a scent of her breath, or hear the fluttering of her eyelashes against each other like butterfly wings.

She took in the history of every being that ever took a breath or spoke a word on this street.

Each heartbeat from below thudded through her, from those murdered and buried in shallow graves, now just pictures on missing persons flyers, to the mailmen walking house to house, bag over shoulders. She marveled at the dreams of those who woke up before dawn and bussed to work, walking through the bitter cold mornings, or those fighting against age so they could care for their grandchildren. But when she sensed someone with a demonic past and devilish plan, that was when she fed on the human flesh with the most ferocity, eating enough fat and protein to power herself for the next twenty-eight-day cycle.

The church was prime hunting ground, and like the food pantry of old, the Word of Faith, was still feeding her—only now it was the people inside. She tore up a score of bodies from the congregation, those who were like little cancer cells rotting away at the souls of others who were truly anointed.

She was the chemotherapy.

She was cleansing the world of their sins.

Each time she fed, she ripped the heart out of the body to make sure it would never beat again. Nobody could have her blessing and curse. She traveled through the shadows behind parked cars, overgrown brush, or dashing up utility poles, feeling the power of 100,000 volts surge through her, moving through zip codes, waiting for the scent of her child. She would never stop the search to find that part of her that was taken away. Sometimes she wanted to travel the country and give chase to find her baby, but the stronger spark in her brain told her to stay put, to be patient. The salmon will come back upstream to home, to where she was born.

Maya walked by the church at times in her depression, sometimes sitting inside listening to the new preacher. The new pastor had meticulously crafted hair, jawbones clearly defined when he spoke words with conviction. He preached with passion while the large brown cross behind him acted as his backbone. He did his best to ignite the crowd to return, because after the numerous closed-casket funerals, Maya saw fewer and fewer people coming to church.

Maya still attended sometimes in the quiet, but largely made her lair in the house her daddy bought. Tiny flakes of his dead skin cells were still part of the dust, still on the hardwood floor, still stuck within the paint on the walls. It was enough to make it seem he still lived inside. She didn't need the urn full of Daddy's ashes any longer.

She had unfinished business at Owl's Party Store, and the man who'd always been afraid to even graze her flesh when offering her up change. It was just before midnight when she visited, right after a manic transition and her body started to sizzle with power, her eyes detecting motion, her nose detecting fear, legs built to bound at prey, sharpened teeth and nails to cleave. The men who stood by the side of the store dropped their bagged bottles when they saw the goddess of the night approach. The bottles shattered on the ground and they dashed off to other places.

Inside the party store, Owl's eyes froze in disbelief, the

way so many do the moment they see her. Before he could move she reached over the counter, through the bulletproof glass, scattering the packets with *Maximum Sexual Performance* written across in neon letters, knocking one of the butane lighters shaped like a skull to the ground. She could taste his hate for people like her, and she refused to consume him, but left his carcass with chest cavity burrowed out and empty on the floor.

Security cameras captured video of it all, but she was unrecognizable, and the police looked for the monster in the city, but never looked for her. Never went to her abandoned childhood home nor looked inside the basement of the church where she still held service with her own memories.

She washed herself off when the depression hit, watching the blood swirl in brooks as she waded. Or she showered in cold water, soaking her muscles that faded back into their original state as the bones crackled into place underneath.

She thought of visiting Lilith's father again, the man who tried to protect his child by killing her. Maybe they could make another child together. He was the only man who could lay with her when she became wet with desire, the only one who could survive long enough, who's chest she could not rip open in her rapture.

But to create another child would be to forget her first.

Most of her mood swings and transitions were the same, but in the days of July a depression came that was deeper than the rest, where she wished she could end this cycle of madness. She lay for days dreaming of how she could stop living and visit her mother, who must miss her and long for her. But even if she did fill herself with poisonous pesticide, it wouldn't work. It would do nothing.

The mania that awoke her from this sleep seemed to run red, like electrical wires filled with lava, surging through her brain, infusing her with a power that burned. Her depression was shattered unlike ever before. Her soul and spine vibrated with energy. Muscles surging, clarity and mania summoned forth, sizzling away her old skin. She shed her old self and left it on the floor, then climbed through the second story window to stand on the roof of her house.

On the horizon, just over the buildings, the moon appeared gigantic, one huge eye of God peeking at his creations over the edge of Earth. Its crimson hue seeped over the aqua blue. The soothing celestial eye in the sky was now a ferocious red that coated the world. The world was going to bleed.

God was she driven and focused.

She jumped off the roof and landed with legs that immediately sprang into a run. So many delicious new scents in the air with the blood-red supermoon, and the one scent she had waited for filled her with supreme ecstasy.

Her daughter. Lilith was near.

She could sense it for the first time in over a dozen years, the unmistakable smell of her flesh, *their shared flesh*, and a shared condition. This new species she'd become, something so hideous and glorious, no normal human could withstand, for whoever walks the earth with this gift, walks alone.

Until now.

With each frenetic step closer, the scent got stronger, and Maya was sure the blood vessels in her brain would burst, that her muscles would rip apart from her bones, and by the time she reached Lilith, she'd be just a spine and a soul, completely stripped bare.

The trail led her through familiar streets to the abandoned building—the church called the Word of Faith.

From the outside, she could see the church was lit. A few candles glowed inside, and near the flame, she sensed her blessed child, raging brighter than the tiny lit fire.

Praise God. Praise Jesus. Maya started to praise them all— all the divine beings, the spiritual healers, the bodhisattvas who walked the earth, the saints and the angels and the discarded demons, for to see her daughter again was to see the face of God.

But instead of joy, it felt like barb wire had been thread through her blood vessels, for Maya could sense tears. Wails. Anguish from inside.

Cries of pain from her daughter were leaking from inside the building and cutting apart Maya's own flesh. Lilith was indeed in the church, but she wasn't safe, and she wasn't alone.

No time to open doors, so Maya burst through a window. The explosion of glass followed, little glass diamonds sprinkling to the ground. Maya landed on the floor and took in the scene around her.

There, at the front of the church, was her child.

Lilith, the original woman, banished for the more respectable Eve.

When Maya saw her, she had to arch her back and raise her jaws to release the howl of joy and pain, of rage and anger, because the brown cross that stood before the church was no longer an empty cross as intended.

It was now a crucifix.

Lilith was tied to the cross. Her arms were extended outward from her body, and her feet tied below. No longer the infant, she was a young woman, much like Maya. Primal, savage and so beautiful. Her muscles smooth, her scent so sweet, her aura full of glowing wisdom. Her eyes sparkled, but were partly covered by droopy eyelids. There was sadness, perpetual pain.

Those lips had fed from her breast. That body and soul had grown inside her, but then grew up outside of her reach. Now crucified.

Rather than nails pounded into her flesh, syringes had been nailed into her skin. A needle stuck out of each arm, two more stuck out of her feet.

And one syringe stuck directly in the center of her chest.

Maya howled again, piercing the walls, piercing the floor, summoning every demon from Hell who might be conjured to fight such curse.

She was not alone in this room.

She turned to looked at the tall woman, the doctor, standing there aiming a weapon towards Maya's gut. Her blood turned leaden. She remembered this silver liquid, not just in her thoughts, but her body. She remembered its weight in her veins, how it dulled her senses and melted her mind and chained her gifts.

Maya could feel the woman's fingers caress the trigger,

ready to fire.

Maya howled again, a lion's roar, and would have coupled her battle cry with furious and deadly attack if not for this deadly substance taking aim.

Maya stared into the doctor's eyes, and memories of the doctor's life seeped into her head. Memories of times Doctor Zita had spent with Lilith, bathing her as a child, feeding her, putting her to sleep and watching over her. She was there for Lilith's first steps, taken so early in her life, and heard her first words. The two had traveled the country to the west and camped out under the vast sky of Yosemite Park. They had heard the stars burning, smelled the embers of their death, watched in wonder at the burning gas still shooting light from far away galaxies into their eyes.

All these experiences that this woman stole from Maya, that were meant to be hers.

And Maya could hear the lies that the doctor had told Lilith, feeding her with false words; "*Your mom hurt you. Your mom gave you a sickness. The universe is going to make her suffer for what she did to you.*" And then always injecting Lilith with the silver liquid, making sure she could not know her full beauty.

Maya sensed this whole history, and it fueled her rage at the woman who stood before her.

"I truly am sorry for this Maya," the doctor said. "I needed to get your attention, needed to get you here to this church."

Maya tried to speak on the betrayal, but the words came out once again in a scream rather than human words.

"I have not lied to you. I have given you what I promised, what you always wanted. I hope you see that you were always right, even if others didn't believe you. You are the Mother of the Messiah. Your instinct was correct all along, and we have to sacrifice our daughter to save the world. On the cross is the only proper way for saviors such as her to die."

Maya felt her mouth open by instinct. She flashed her sharpened teeth and ached for the taste of warm blood and vengeance. Her daughter needed to come down from the cross.

Maya started pacing in circles around the woman, and as she did the doctor tracked her with the tranquilizer gun loaded with Luminex.

"I do care for you, Maya. In some ways, you and I are family, for *I* am with child. A child borne from Lilith's womb, of her first eggs. They were fertilized by a man with similar might, an immaculate conception, and this new birth will be an even more powerful and perfect human. A mental illness fixed, so not an illness any longer."

The woman spoke with pride, but Maya felt fear release from each pore of her skin. She was scared, and in turn the muscles of her index finger clenched, ready to fire.

"I gave this power to you Maya. Now I have to take it away."

Rather than attack the doctor, Maya sprung into action towards Lilith, darting towards the crucifix. She made it to the foot of the cross, and with one hand, plucked a syringe out of her child's foot. She had to save her, take her down from the cross, the silver was killing her.

Thwack.

A dart hit Maya's back and the Luminex seeped into her muscles. She felt the energy leaving her body, the familiar sedative effect. She fell to the ground, Mary Magdalene at the foot of Jesus.

She gazed up at the beautiful child on the cross.

God, why have you done this? Why let this happen?

Maya prayed she could be nailed to the cross alongside Lilith, immortalized in an embrace, then the two could harrow Hell together, just like Jesus. Instead she had to watch her suffer. She tried to sense a heartbeat from her daughter's chest, but could detect none. *She's dead. Dying. There has never been a girl so forsaken.* Her pupils had disappeared. The droopy eyelids fully closed and covered them.

Come on, open your eyes, look into mine, one last time, one last time.

Maya tried to stand but could not. The silver spreading through her body was pulling her down, so she grabbed the base of the wooden cross, trying to rise herself up, unbound the ropes, and pull her child down. She had her daughter's calf, felt her tender skin for just a brief moment, sensing all the history inside, but then...

Thwack.

Another syringe stuck in her flesh, shot by Zita, this time sticking out of her hamstring, and it brought her to the ground, lying there broken, tortured by the sight of her daughter above.

It was not supposed to be like this.

The doctor loomed over her and looked down, her hair falling at her sides, her eyes so cold and blue.

"Truth is, this is the best way for you both to be together, to die side by side. What can be better than that?"

27

LILITH ON THE CROSS

The board of directors scheduled emergency meetings after the Word of Faith killings. They hired a PR director. They held fundraisers and charity drives to pay for the funerals. There were stories in the paper, there were segments in the local news. The church seemed it might survive the declining congregation and dwindling numbers when media coverage led to bountiful donations.

But after entrails were left, and bodies were found with chests excavated, when security guards were killed, the body of worshippers started to find other houses of worship. Scheduled services went from two on Sunday to only one. The killings continued, month after month, and legends grew about the curse of Pastor Ronald Pennington.

When the church finally closed, it was only meant to be temporary until the killer was found.

"We have many leads."

"We have a person of interest."

"We have an arrest. The suspect is in custody!"

It became clear they had the wrong suspect when the board president was found with his limbs dismembered and unexplained cash in his bank accounts. He had not been paying on their lease, but diverting to his own Venmo account, and the church defaulted on their loan. They had stopped paying the electric, stopping paying the water, and had to auction off furniture.

They didn't think it right to auction off the wooden cross, which still stood tall in the church. With the church abandoned and lit up by candles, the crucified body of a twelve-year-old girl cast a flickering shadow on the back wall.

Lilith had felt the stab of each metallic syringe punctured inside her. The same syringes that had been poked into her thigh for years, but now they were ripping her open and making her heart cry in tears of lead. Her eyes were about to close for good, her final vision of the world was this woman, her true mother, being attacked at her feet. Her heavy eyelids kept dropping and she was unable to break free from the cross.

Why have you done this to me?

As a little girl living on the west coast, Lilith imagined that it was love that made Mama Z inject her with medicine. So many times, she had smelled the vanilla lotion on Mama Z's skin, looked into her blue eyes and thought to herself, *See, you are loved. Your sickness is being tended to,* but now she felt the burn of the silver metal, ready to turn her insides to stone, and knew she was being fooled all along.

For twelve years she was fooled, and it wasn't until she was left alone in that cheap motel room that her true self emerged, reborn, and she then returned to her real birthplace. Spit out of a volcano eruption, and landed like a new species inside a strange, frightening body and expansive mind.

When she had arrived at her birthing room in the hospital dungeon, she felt such sadness for the creatures still trapped in the basement, so had released them from their chains. They had been bound, just like her, in a sense, but upon release, she knew they were not like her. They were ready to destroy and spread their disease. They were nasty and bitter souls. Lilith had a vision of the vengeful creatures destroying the world by feeding and spreading their curse in their path.

Mistakes, all of them, is what Mama Z had said. *Things that should not be. The by-product of all the hurt inside those hospital walls.*

After the basement beings were unbound and her power was waning, Lilith had summoned the energy to climb from the tunnels, but then dropped to the ground outside the hospital. She could barely move, her energy gone, when a sister named Kori had saved her and brought her home, tried to hide her. But the woman called Mama Z was a serpent, slithering into her hiding spot, and took her away.

"I'm sorry," Zita had said to Lilith at the last moment and stared into her face, just inches away. Lilith felt herself drowning in the icy blue artic sea of Zita's eyes. The final deep puncture into her heart had ripped her soul open, split her spine in two. She had gasped for breath, one last gulp of air, and then froze in place, hanging lifeless and tied to the cross.

She hung there with her heart full of silver and no longer beating with her mom at her feet,

Death at first felt like ascending, like flying up into the glowing heat and piercing flames of the sun, and then falling to earth, stuck back on the cross where a vulture swooped down and picked at her side, eating her liver. Then her body seemed to burn in a river of fire, before spiraling down to a place inside her spine, through the hallows of the earth, through the time before machinery and cities, beyond the idea that a human can commit a sin.

She watched the first humans living and hunting in tribes, savage and saintly, the most sentient and gifted creation on earth. None of them wore any clothes, the idea of shame so foreign, only feeding and breeding while the moon shined down on them, glistening with blood and sweat and milk. Their senses acute beyond measure and the dimensions of the world lay before them in full splendor.

Lilith wanted to join them, her own tribe, with her own mother.

God how she longed to be in her mom's embrace, her real mom, who was laying on the church floor and being murdered. If she could just get her own heart to start beating again.

You found me, Mom, we were so close, but instead we will die together.

The ocean of moonlight-blue shining down and illuminating the first humans turned into blood-red, and she witnessed a new kind of death among them—death by murder. Humans and tribes turned on each other in fear, betraying and forsaking and torturing. Brother killing brother, and sister destroying sister.

She wanted to escape the cross but she could not. Her legs wouldn't move, her heart wouldn't beat, her arms were stuck, tied to the wood and pierced with needles.

Lilith wept.

She heard the words of Jesus echo from his own crucifixion, stuck on the ancient torture device. Unlike her, his eyes opened, and he ripped his bloody body off the cross and took her by the hand and led her downward.

She was taken down to a cavern of burning souls, those who had been treated by good intentions, but devilish results. Those with brilliant minds, whose synapses fired with powers unknown to most human kind. Suffering souls with misunderstood gifts, who sang together in a harmony of torture that vibrated her ears and echoed inside the basement of every psychiatric facility of all time.

The pain on their faces became the new nails of her crucifixion. She felt their hurt when their family beat them and banished them in frustration. Communities feared them, and they were forced into hurtful care. Blood-sucking leeches were stuck on their skin, exorcism rituals performed in their rooms, their brains disconnected by lobotomy doctors, their hands were tied to bedframes, they were stuck in seclusion rooms. Many wished for death. Their silent screams went unheard, a language not understood.

But Lilith did understand, she was harrowing hell, and here to save them. To gather their power to use for her own.

The first recognizable soul was that of her own grandmother. Maya's mother. Her ancestor's face was aged, weathered, tired. She had swallowed pesticide, the only thing she thought would kill the bugs that burrowed through her brain. The pesticide worked — it had killed the bugs that had nested in her mind, but also killed her body and left her in eternity with a soul full of hateful poison.

"You are loved," Lilith whispered to her lonely grandma. "You are loved. I know this, I felt it in your daughter, the one you never met, but who thinks of you just the same."

The pesticide started to bubble, boil, and then evaporate, compelled to leave her grandmother's body and stop poisoning her spirit. The memories of the two fused and become one in communion.

She approached the body of her father, Peter Driscoe, recently put to sleep and trapped within the first layer of hell below the hospital. His hands were folded on his chest and he was surrounded by the beasts who had haunted him his entire life. He was being buried under crumbling concrete that came crashing down on him, his final resting place. He'd lived as Medusa had, for every person he'd ever cared for, every person he laid eyes upon with love, the relationships had all turned cold as a stone.

The memory of his hands squeezing her neck as an infant still pressed against her jugular. He'd been trying to prevent her suffering, and she had stared back into his eyes full of sorrow. He only wanted to bring her a peace he never had the only way he knew how. The best of intentions, the worst of results.

Now they were dead together, and she whispered into his ear.

"You are loved."

His sleep was in peace. Each bit of his DNA that she still carried in her own body sparked in fits of eternal flames. His death was an illusion. He was immortal.

The Medusa had found his Messiah.

Lilith's spirit then became surrounded by smoke drifting from the front porch of a sad, little home. It was from Doctor Zita's mom's last cigarette. The smoke drifted high in the air as if her spirit was burning in her body, her soul cremated, her flesh and bones just the urn for the ashes. The odor was that of a human rotting.

The smoke cleared, and the woman gagged, then vomited. Sirens from the heavens rang, ambulances or devils, and digested bits wiggled like germs on a bedspread.

"I took them all for her. I took every last pill," Zita's mom said. "I couldn't fix me. I tried. She wanted to fix me. She tried so hard, so she made you."

You didn't need fixing. Lilith tried to say, but didn't need to, because the woman felt the words.

Soon a full army came forth out of their deeper layers of Hell. They came from the cracks in the hospital concrete, from their places of suicide, of depression, of psychotic torment that would not stop. Their brains and souls burning with such hurt, rarely doused with understanding and tenderness, instead with fear and foolish consistency.

Lilith didn't fear them — she *was* them, and she harrowed the murkiest layers she could find, summoning more forth; men, woman, children, generations who've suffered.

Come into me, Lilith thought, and they did. The whole of their pain and anguish was invited to show itself, and she soaked in their sickness and powers through the hundreds of pinholes Zita had put into her body.

Lilith felt herself back on the wooden cross, with her mom on the ground before her, just seconds until she was killed and joined those suffering in abandoned parts of Hell.

But Lilith was changed.

This medication can't stop me anymore.

Her soul began to sing with new power, her spirit to glow. The new energy in her heart pumped the thick, red plasma and it moved through her veins again, back the way it came. Her heart was an engine powered by coal of the deepest hells. It fought back against the tainted silver liquid. Pushing it. Forcing it. Making it retreat and return to the tiny syringe needles stuck in her body, back into the cartridge, and out of her altogether.

Her left arm was first to break free from the cross, sending the syringe out of the muscle and onto the ground, raining down to the nearby Doctor Zita. Lilith's hand now free, she snatched the syringe impaled in her chest, felt the tug on her heart as she pulled, and she ripped it free. The blood-soaked tip was tossed aside. Next, her right arm, then her legs kicked forth.

She was set free, unbound from that which crucified her, and she landed on the ground before the cross and sang a song of praise to the sky. The blood-red moon bore witness.

With Doctor Zita ready to plunge the Luminex into her real mother's heart, Lilith acted with rage and precision. She swiped at Zita's arm, ripping the skin, tearing the ligaments, once again — same as her mom had done over a dozen years prior. Zita's arm was rendered useless, and the deadly syringe fell to the ground.

Zita opened her blue eyes in cold disbelief, and Lilith swiped again at her neck, a razor-thin slice. The blood no longer rushed to the doctor's head, but out her jugular. It puddled at the base of the cross.

Lilith looked into Zita's ice-blue eyes as she lay on the ground, slowly losing consciousness, dying but not yet dead.

"Kill me," Zita managed words. "Go ahead and kill me. And when you do, know that you also kill your own child. Our child."

Lilith could sense this was true and not another one of her lies. She could hear the tiny egg's heart beating inside the doctor's body, alive and nestled in her womb. Lilith placed a palm on the wound on her neck, waiting for a clot, wanting to punish this woman to eternal Hell, but to somehow save the presence inside.

Then to her own mother's body.

Maya lay safely on the ground, and Lilith burrowed her body beside her. The daughter's head rested on her mother's chest, and she was once again part of her host, her mind asleep but her body still warm and vibrant. They soaked in each other's history and memory as if they had never been separated. A church of renewed faith and reunited family.

28

Kori Trapped in the Tunnels

Kori took a sip of water and let it soak into her lips and pool around her tongue.

God did it feel good to keep the water in her parched mouth, but as soon as she took a sip, her stomach begged her to swallow.

Each cell of her body was craving for water, for food, for hope.

She had stopped checking for a way out. All had been blocked.

All exits were full of rubble. Even the tunnel leading up to the surface by climbing up the metal rungs wasn't an option. A manhole cover at the top was weighted down with hospital debris. That became clear after she spent at least an hour pushing on the first try, another half hour the second try, but it had weight upon it like never before.

A claustrophobic dread hit her some moments. Other times, stoic acceptance, for this felt deserved.

So she returned to sit with her dad's body, making sure his hands were folded peacefully on his chest. His skin had grown cold. Rather than rot, he seemed to be turning into a silver statue from the elixir injected into his heart.

Kori sipped on water from the jug, imagining she could live for a few weeks like this. She ate just tiny bits of Snickers at a time, sharing a bit with Hades, who then licked the wrappers clean. Her very brain hurt, delirium was coming by degrees. She rubbed the right side of her head, just above the ear. Her hair hadn't been shaved down in quite a while. She hated when it grew out, loved the moments when it was trimmed down to reveal her scalp. She cherished the memory of her dad's palm scraping against it in the hours after a fresh cut.

Hades was hungry for something more and constantly sniffing about. She finally trotted over, head hung low, and nibbled on the rib cage of the security guard. Kori turned her head, not wanting Hades to feel any more shame, for the dog could be forgiven any trespasses at this moment. Kori wished she could help the animal understand, *This is not your fault, this is my fault.*

Hades returned to Kori's side with bloody jowls.

Kori watched over the sleeping little goblin creatures and as her stomach emptied, her head filled with memories. There was no day or night down here.

She left the room at times for a walk, and roamed the tunnels like she roamed her own history in her head, both of them full of dead-ends. Always she came back to the same room as if she would find something new, but it remained the tomb of her dad, dead amongst the creatures. The *Vrykolakas*, he called them. She had already lived with these things for years, only now they had become visible. It was much too late to matter, but she thought of ways to slay these beasts.

She watched them sleep as a parent might a child, becoming intimately acquainted with each one. All had pig-like skin, mutated bodies, one with an arm that split into two hands, and she imagined it now as having three weapons — two hands and its jaw. Another had just two holes on its face instead of nostrils, and below that, its mouth was stuck in a full grin as if the creature was living inside a blissful dream. Another wheezed for air with every breath, every second a struggle, like its internal organs were so twisted up inside. Each moment alive was suffering.

She should kill that one first.

One Vrykolakas was cursed with an uncloseable eye, and seemed the most insidious. The eye was covered with a pink film and had no eyelid. Kori felt a shiver of coldness when she gazed at its pupil, pointing the flashlight to its side so that the pale light barely spilled over its face and didn't awaken the creature.

Kori had been under the tunnels for a couple of weeks when she finally pulled out her knife with plans to stab one in the heart. They needed to be put down. She knew she'd have to gouge the knife deeply, enough to destroy the beating heart inside. She held the metal blade to its chest, same as she had with syringe to her dad, but this time she didn't stop. She punctured deep into its chest with all her might.

The metal was sharp, the Target product was well made, and she watched the little Vrykolakas open its eyes, for just a split second, wanting to fight back, but death snatched it before it had the chance.

It didn't wake the others.

She killed another a few days later.

This is what happens in this room, people die here. She was going to be buried next to her dad. The empty feeling of hunger and thirst could not be fought back with sips of water or nibbles of candy. Hades was also running out of scraps.

The demolition seemed to have moved on to other buildings, and she wondered how much was completed. She knew they were not going to implode the building, but instead take down the walls first. Too much industrial waste to blow it to bits. Her car wasn't far — had it been discovered? She imagined detectives, experts at tracking, sensing her steps through the Evil Woods, maybe some of her blood had fallen and a dog would sniff her scent. And then a hero would unbury her after they realized she was trapped.

It was going to take a savior.

The wounds on her face — one from Lilith, one from the Vrykolakas — were dirty and definitely infected. They started to spread deeper into her flesh, traveling down her veins, up her spine, into her brain. God, did the wounds itch, and when it became too much, she peeled back the scabs from her face. Her mouth watered when she placed the scab on her tongue. The taste of her own plasma and clotted blood. She needed more.

Hunger was eating up her insides.

She fell into sleep, curled up with a restless Hades. Death of some sort was coming. Her body started to dissipate, her skin bubbling beneath its surface and ready to be shed and discarded. Her stomach was empty, but her senses full, engorged and overflowing. She started to hear every bit of motion, the tiniest flutter of a limb in the room, the remains of the security guard decaying. The flashlight was no longer needed, for she was able to see through the darkness that had become grey.

She was awakened with a new energy, so vibrant, and so delicious to her empty gut. Something inside her was trying to crawl its way out of her skin and take Kori over. Muscles she never knew she had were rising.

They were also wakening. The Vrykolakas no longer slept.

The first one leapt for her, and in a flash of primal instinct, Kori raised up her hand and reacted. She caught the creature in the air by its neck, and flung it against the wall. Its head smacked the concrete, and it fell to the ground, stunned and momentarily harmless.

Kori had grown strong with rage, with vitality, growing with each moment. She detected the beasts' every motion, and sense the temperature change in the room as the creatures woke form their sleep.

She knew she'd have to fight or get eaten.

There were so many. The eye that could not close was no longer asleep, and the pupil that moved burned into her. They were ready to hunt as a group, spreading out as a pack of wolves might around a wounded deer.

Hades barked at them, went in circles, ran towards the exit, back to face them down, back to the exits again. Kori had the same instinct to flee, for she knew could not face all of them.

She ran from the room, and all of them followed. They left Hades alone.

We don't care about the dog, we want the person, the human, it was humans who created us and chained us here.

A score of them gave chase, all of them propelled by their DNA full of trauma and an unquenchable thirst to feed. Kori moved through the tunnel like never before, a bat flying with radar through the dark. Where to go, she wasn't certain, but instinct dashed her alongside the pipes of this dungeon, through the hall, and then to the rungs leading upward, up the cement tube. So fast to the top, the spot where she had pushed on with all her might so many times before, but now she was different. Stronger. Primitive muscles powered her.

The round cylinder moved.

In all her new strength, she could move it.

Below her was high-pitched growling, like a group of hyenas waiting for a treat. Above her, the sound of the metal manhole scraping against concrete. She grunted, moving it aside, summoning all her strength, pushing it, just a bit, just a bit more, until...

It all came crashing down.

Rather than space to escape, after just the briefest bit of night air, she had caused an avalanche. A waterfall of concrete from the destroyed hospital rained down upon her. It smashed against her head, ripped open her skin, and piled up all around.

She was buried. Buried in the ruins, and she groaned and pushed with every muscle, but was stuck immobile in the concrete.

She could feel the night sky tugging at her, the moon beckoning her to rise up, but the chunks of cement that for years had housed thousands of suffering souls, now had her trapped.

The damage caused by the concrete would have killed most, but not her. She lay there fully conscious for hours. Even though she could not breathe, she also could not die. She tried to call for help, but then she realized that the graffiti on the wall was right.

You Can't Scream With Your Lungs Full of Dirt

She pressed against the rocks and concrete, and any bit that budged only resettled the humongous weight above. She imagined what floors this cement was from. She could sense traces of floor eight, of floor three, of concrete slabs direct from the sunroof on top. All of it was now her casket. A tomb she now shared with her dad.

Hell isn't a place, it's being stuck alive in times like this.

An eternity went by. She wasn't even breathing but her thoughts were still looping, soaking in the history of the hospital in the concrete that buried her, feeling each moment. Finally, she felt something move above her. The crane. It must have returned, because things were shifting. Something was trying to reach her, she hoped to pull her to safety.

Just a dream. The same reoccurring nightmare of her life.

The nightmare where she had felt the grasp of her dad's hand upon her arm and could sense the sting of his disease in every pore. He was yanking against her arm, like the night of *the incident*, hurting her shoulder. The socket of her shoulder clicked in pain, but it was a memory cherished. Dad was trying so hard to save her with intentions full of love. He was grabbing her and pulling her and bringing her to whatever heaven or hell he'd been delivered to in the afterlife.

Her mom didn't understand it and called the police, who got in the way. And then hospitals kept them apart.

Take me to your hell, Dad, she thought, hoping he would keep yanking until she split in two.

And her dad did answer, for she was being pulled from the wreckage.

As if spit out of the volcano, she landed on the earth a completely new being.

She coughed out chunks of dirt, took her first breath of outside air in days, and then stared into the eyes of her savior. It was not her dad who pulled her out, but her sister—her half-sister, her dad's child, who had grabbed her arm and saved her. The magnificent and majestic girl named Lilith, who Kori had carried to her car a month earlier, had now pulled her from her own grave and set her upon the earth under the night sky.

Kori was left lying on the grounds of the crumbling Northville Psychiatric, bathing under the moonlight. Her whole body burned and sizzled, and she was coated with sediment from the hospital that would never come clean.

Shortly after, Lilith descended down into the tunnel, and then rose up the rungs carrying Hades over her shoulder. Hades came and sniffed Kori, full of sweetness, but shortly after her, a score of other beings came pouring out from the hole in the ground.

The Vrykolakas, set free.

For just a moment, the wretched beast with the perpetually open eye stared into Lilith. The pale film over the pupil changed shades while its stare sized up her enemy. It gave a quick growl, which was met with Lilith's savage roar, and then it ran off with the rest of the pack into the Evil Woods.

The three of them, Kori, Lilith, and Hades, were safe. Soon after, they left the crumbling hospital and ran into the tree line, led by Lilith. They sliced through the Evil Woods. They moved in the shadows of the blood-red moon, on their way to the Word of Faith.

Inside the church, the cross had fallen to its side, the strings of rope still partially tied upon it, but loosened. All the seats were empty. The savagely wounded body of Doctor Zita had been discovered and taken, but Maya was there waiting.

They all lived and hunted together for one full night under the blood-red moon, howling in unison, in harmony, with boundless energy and strength. And when the moon waned, their mania waned. Hades stood guard while Lilith, Kori and Maya slept in the basement of the abandoned church, feeling it breathe, feeling it speak, a month of dreams. A coma of depression.

Twenty-eight days later, the light of the moon tugged at their hearts and awoke them into the aqua-blue night. Their bones stretched and crackled, expanding with the size and strength of raging mania and pulsating muscles. Their senses soaked in the spectrum of stimuli no other human could sense. The first scent they detected was the freshly wakened Vrykolakas, miles away but still alive. Still hungry, still angry — always angry.

The Vrykolakas sensed them as well, and in each moment, they moved closer.

The full moon would soon witness the inevitable battle.

And in a hospital bed nearby, Doctor Zita's pregnant body was intubated and on life support, but the child inside had grown to full gestation in her womb, ready for birth, ready to breathe on its own.

About the Author

Mark Matthews is a graduate of the University of Michigan and a licensed professional counselor who has worked in behavioral health for over 20 years. He is the author of On the Lips of Children, Body of Christ, All Smoke Rises, and Milk-Blood. He is the editor of, and a contributor to, Lullabies for Suffering and Garden of Fiends. He lives near Detroit with his family. Reach him at WickedRunPress@gmail.com

Afterword, From the Author

Who actually reads the afterword? Why, you do! That's who, and thank you for doing so. The content from this novel begs a brief discussion. A few points of clarity regarding psychotropic medications, bipolar disorder, and a note on the setting.

I wrote The Hobgoblin of Little Minds with the perpetual concern and sensitivity that I could be adding to the burden of those living with mental illness rather than offering empathy and understanding. Similar to my works of addiction horror, there was a risk of stigmatizing those impacted by the disorder, versus shining a light into their lives. I sought out beta readers to gauge the tone and representation, and found, as I hoped, that the message was received as intended. Of course, this will not be true for all readers, but *fiction should be dangerous or nothing at all.* One of those dangers is that I perhaps missed one crucial message:

Medications and psychiatric treatment saves lives. Doctors do care.

I believe in mental health treatment. I believe in talk therapy and psychotropic medications. I believe medications work and have witnessed the life-improvement that can come from finely tuned medications.

All of the above is true, but not always true, and not true enough of the time. Too often we minimize the consumer's experience and the side effects of medications. We want others to take the medications for our own purposes, and disregard the full spectrum of their impact. Those who take psychotropic meds often feel they are losing themselves even as the devastating symptoms are alleviated. It can feel like you are losing your gifts and what makes you unique. Rather than seen as an act of self-care, to take medications can cause feelings of inferiority — like evidence that you are not capable to direct your own life. Even when medications are at their most effective, it can feel dehumanizing to need them in order to not decompensate. To cease medications can feel an act of bravery, and as much as that's a false belief, we need to understand that rather than demonize it.

Innovations like peer supports in community mental health and patients' bill of rights help create a more dignifying course of treatment. Research into the role of the gut in the treatment of depression and anxiety and non-invasive treatment such as Transcranial Magnetic Stimulation (TMS) are exciting new trends.

My take on medications has evolved, and will always be evolving. Twenty years ago, I felt that to use suboxone in order to discontinue heroin use was not really recovery. Fast forward to today, and I've recommended suboxone plenty, even as maintenance, for harm reduction.

Some personal experience has also opened my eyes. I started an anti-depressant used for nerve pain, and what it did shocked me. The only way I can describe it is that *thoughts hurt — to even have a thought — hurt*. My thoughts were stuck in an agonizing loop. I've also taken what is normally seen as a sleeper, Trazadone, for insomnia and it made me so much worse. My eyes popped open after two hours of sleep, my brain in a fog and my body unable to sleep for another 24 hours. *No way*, was I going to take that medication again. It did not feel safe. But if I were a mental health patient, I'd be called non-compliant. Yet I know that patients are directed to keep pushing through.

Medications work so differently for each person that at times it seems an *experiment of one* with consequences hard to predict. Very often the conditions targeted are made worse. This happens frequently with Bipolar Disorder where mania is triggered by anti-depressants.

The symptoms of Bipolar as presented in this novel are certainly of the more extreme in nature, but they are not uncommon in their occurrence. The psychosis, the agitation, the grandiosity, insomnia, hyper-sexuality, tangential thoughts, loose association, engaging frenetically in activities that have painful consequences— all of this is incredibly common. Beyond my twenty years working in behavioral health, before I wrote this work, I read numerous accounts of living with the bipolar in books such as *Manic: A Memoir,* by Terri Cheney, and *Fast Girl: A Life Spent Running from Madness,* by Suzy Favor Hamilton.

So many revered artists and personalities we admire have manic episodes, and there seems a risk when *mania* itself is romanticized. While it comes with euphoria and an elated mood, it is not a pleasant experience, typically, but a flurry of thought and energy which can't be satisfied. Any actual productively is marked by something destructive. The often-ensuing depression makes one feel mocked by memories of previous levels of energy.

The premise of werewolf as a metaphor for these mood swings is a concept that was with me for years, and after I researched the topic, I found I was not alone.

"When I Became A Werewolf," (Ohio State University, 2015) a research thesis by Via Laurene Smith speaks to this very topic. Laurene Smith explores how monsters are a "mechanism manifested to deal with human fears, including the fear of mental illness. They originated as horrific dangerous beasts who couldn't control their unstable tendencies and needed to be locked away or destroyed, much like the early ways of dealing with people who suffered from mental illness." In her personal, brave, and fantastic thesis she, "investigates the parallels between depictions of the werewolf and that of bipolar disorder and depression and asks to what extent the werewolf can be

used to reflect or even change attitudes towards mental illness."

Another scholarly article that speaks directly to the topic is, "*Folklore perpetuated expression of moon-associated bipolar disorders in anecdotally exaggerated werewolf guise,*" published by the University Hospital of Cologne, authors, Thomas C. Erren, Philip Lewis (2018).

The article hypothesizes that "Moon-associated signals, recently linked to rapid cycling bipolar disorder, may have triggered extremely rare instances of extreme manic and aggressive behavior that may be compatible with the folklore of the werewolf."

The article certainly does not conclude that the moon literally causes lycanthropy, but instead suggests: "Rather than ignoring folklore, scientists may want to think what biological roots may manifest in folklore tradition and tales. Such awareness could fuel new insights and benefit causal understanding for individuals and populations in regards to the roots, causes, and significance of health and disease-associated traditions and tales, including the werewolf legend."

In other words, the best way to tell the truth sometimes is through a work of horror.

Horror and folklore usually come from truth, just an exaggerated version or as metaphor. Japan really was destroyed by a fire-breathing monster, though atomic bombs, not Godzilla, was the vehicle of the devastating delivery. Townspeople really are terrified of the aristocrat in the castle, even if Vlad Dracula doesn't change into a bat. And werewolves really do represent a dark, savage part of us. As my professor Eric Rabkin from University of Michigan explained, "Werewolves were often considered the villains in the forest. The Jungian self gone wild."

I hope this story has added to the legend of werewolves, which in some ways is a forgotten trope and archetype over the last few decades which has seen the rise of vampires first, then zombies second. That is now changing. The moon is full and it's now the time of the wolf. Look no further than Mongrels, by Stephen Graham Jones.

A final note about the setting. I've done hours of research

into Northville Psychiatric Hospital. The place was legendary in my local community. There is verity in how this setting is presented. There were indeed tunnels connecting the various buildings, and the facility does have all the different rooms and capacity as described. It was a designated bomb shelter and asbestos and hazardous waste complicated its demolition. Locals did call the surrounding area "The Evil Woods," a name derived from The Evil Dead films and created by Michigan native Sam Raimi.

Those who are intimately familiar with the abandoned compound, however, will certainly find something that may not fit — *this building doesn't have this part*, or *this is not that far from that*. I hope you forgive me my minor trespasses.

The city of Northville built numerous state facilities on their land. I was amazed when I realized that Hawthorne Center, still open and treating adolescents, was built on the same parcel as Northville, under a two mile walk away. I liken it to Helen finding the identical Cabrini Green across the highway in Candyman.

In this sense, the work is historical horror, and I reached out to Alma Katsu, (Author of The Hunger and current master of historical horror) who suggested I take a tour of the building. That was no longer possible, since the hospital is now demolished, but I have parked at Hawthorne Center in the very spot Kori Driscoe parked her Toyota before walking through the evil woods to Northville Psychiatric. The land between is now developed, but it wasn't when Kori took her pilgrimages to the dark underground.

I invite you to take a deeper dive and google "Northville Psychiatric Mlive" or "Northville Tunnels Nailhead" for some powerful images and blogs about the facility.

I do hope something from this work lingers, and that it has both entertained and raised questions. The best afterword is forgettable in contrast to the content it follows and vanishes upon reading. Before these words disappear, I want to sincerely thank you for reading them.

ACKNOWLEDGEMENTS

I want to thank a long list of people, but first thanks to my family for living with someone who can become quite obsessed with writing at times. In my best days, it enriches my life to give back with the same vigor (but every day is not my best day). Why do I write like tomorrow won't arrive? I suppose because some day, it won't.

Thanks to the beta readers: Ashley P., Glen Krisch, Johann Thorsson, and Michael Fowler (once again). Huge thanks to Via Laurene Smith, librarian and artist, who was open to such great discussion on the subject as well as a detailed read. Thanks to Tracey Robinson, for her assistance with some research articles. Thanks to Katie C. for some electrifying tips on being a line worker (and the whole ND team for being a constant source of knowledge and enduring my weirdness.) Thanks to Kyle Lybeck for the proofread. Huge gratitude to Julie Hutchings, who has always made my writing beyond something I could ever achieve alone. Thanks to John FD Taff for his book therapy and mentorship. Thanks to a dozen or more book bloggers who are such incredible supports to the horror writing community. Thanks to Kealan Patrick Burke, John Boden, and the late Dallas Mayr. Thanks to professor Eric Rabkin at the University of Michigan, for his lectures on the power of speculative fiction and archetypes. Thanks to Vincent Chong for his amazing artwork and for being such a cool cat.

Lastly, gratitude and thanks to anyone who gave this book a read and spent their precious time inside my dark tunnels. You will escape, but I hope you remember your time spent and agree to return, for this story may not be over just yet.

Made in the USA
Monee, IL
26 January 2021